MONTANA

...where passions run deep and mystery lingers

Welcome to Whitehorn, Montana—the home of bold men and daring women. A place where rich tales of passion and adventure are about to unfold and where one small town has more than its fair share of secrets...

Kyle Mitchell: After two years deep undercover, the FBI agent came home to find his family in danger. Now *nothing* would stop the passionate husband and father from defending his own...

Danielle Mitchell: Danielle didn't want to need Kyle—after all, the sexy secret agent had become a stranger to her during his long disappearance. But how could she deny her daughter his protection?

Sara Mitchell: Little Sara desperately wanted to keep her daddy home safe and sound forever— and complete her family!

D0589687

Dear Reader,

Silhouette® Books is twenty years old and you are going to see lots of top authors appearing in all our series throughout this year. We hope you're going to absolutely adore our anniversary line-up of all your favourite writers, just take a look!

Sherryl Woods gets us off to a flying start with our **That's My Baby!** book, *The Cowboy and the New Year's Baby*, which is the latest addition to her **And Baby Makes Three** mini-series, which is on-going. Also continuing are our **Montana** books, with a wonderful instalment, *A Family Homecoming*, from Laurie Paige who always creates such gorgeous men.

In *A Doctor's Vow* Christine Rimmer starts a new **Prescription: Marriage** trilogy, which is running January-March and each book features a sexy Malone brother and a female physician. With *A Cowboy's Woman*, Cathy Gillen Thacker continues her marvellous **McCabe Men** series, which is coming to you every other month, and Trisha Alexander is revisiting the Callahan family in *Falling For an Older Man*. Finally, we have Carol Finch's second book for us, *Soul Mates*, but she's by no means new to writing, having written more than fifty books and won several awards!

Enjoy them all!

The Editors

PS Don't forget *Fortune's Heirs*, the new stories about the Fortune family, are on sale this month.

A Family Homecoming

LAURIE PAIGE

SILHOUETTE
SPECIAL EDITION

*First published in Great Britain 2001
Silhouette Books, Eton House, 18-24 Paradise Road,
Richmond, Surrey TW9 1SR*

© Harlequin Books S.A. 1999

Special thanks and acknowledgement are given to Laurie Paige for
her contribution to the Montana: Return to Whitehorn series.

ISBN 0 373 24292 1

23-0101

*Printed and bound in Spain
by Litografía Rosés S.A., Barcelona*

LAURIE PAIGE

was presented with the *Affaire de Coeur* Readers'
Choice Silver Pen Award for Favourite Contemporary
Author. In addition, she was a Romance Writers of
America RITA finalist for their Best Traditional
Romance award. She reports romance is blooming in
her part of northern California. With the birth of her
second grandson, she finds herself madly in love with
three wonderful males—'all hero material'. So far, her
husband hasn't complained about the other men in her
life.

MONTANA

...where passions run deep and mystery lingers

Watch for more wonderful, brand-new stories from favourite authors like Laurie Paige, Jennifer Greene, Marilyn Pappano & Linda Turner.

Starting soon with:

The Kincaid Bride from Jackie Merritt

(Silhouette Special Edition -July 2001)

In September look for a complete new series of rich, romantic tales where new heirs to the powerful Kincaid family are found, where a newborn is missing and where murder adds a sense of danger...

Welcome back to Montana—the new generation of tales of passion and adventure capture all the joy and excitement of living and loving!

Chapter One

Home.

Kyle Mitchell stood on the cracked sidewalk in front of the white ramshackle house. Danielle, his wife of six years, had bought it when she'd moved to Whitehorn two years ago. Until this moment he'd never laid eyes on it.

The wind howled forlornly through the evergreens that lined the drive and formed a windbreak against the driving snow. It slid icy fingers under the thick collar of his down-filled parka, roamed down his spine in a series of chillbumps and robbed the heat from his body.

January in Montana was something to be reckoned with.

The lights of the house glowed faintly through the

windows, urging him inside where there would be warmth and human companionship. Still, he lingered.

The letter packed in his luggage didn't invite a rush into the old homestead, which was sort of Victorian, sort of early ranch house style. The twin gables in the steeply pitched roof indicated a second story, perhaps with bedrooms carved out of the attic.

He wondered where Danielle slept.

The longing he'd blocked for two years hit his chest and radiated outward. *Dani,* his heart repeated with each beat. *Dani.*

She wouldn't be glad to see him. The letter proved that. In it, she had said it was time for a divorce. So that they could get on with their lives. So that the uncertainty of their marriage would be resolved. So that they could be entirely free of each other to do whatever they wanted.

What he wanted...her warmth. Her generous love. Her catchy way of laughing. *Dani. Ah, God, Dani.*

The wind rushed down the Crazy Mountains, blew snow in a swirl around his head and blinded him for a moment, bringing the unexpected sting of tears to his eyes. When the gust passed and the air cleared again, he blinked away the flakes that clung to his lashes and stared into the eyes of a young girl. Joy flashed through him.

Sara. His daughter. She'd been three when he'd left two years ago.

Her eyes rounded in obvious fright and her mouth dropped open as if in a silent scream. She spun from the window. The heavy curtains dropped into place behind her, shutting out most of the light.

Stunned, he realized she didn't remember him.

That brought its own remorse, separate from all the other regrets that lingered inside him. If he could go back...

But, once started on a course, life wouldn't let a person go back to Day One and make a better decision. And regret didn't do a damned thing but deepen the pain of loss.

The words of the letter burned in the back of his brain, stamped there for all time, a personal message from Dani to him written on the crumbling wall of their marriage.

I think it best if we consider divorce. I made the down payment on the house from my own savings. Naturally I would like to keep it. Your salary has mostly gone into your savings account. I did have to use some for Sara, clothes and dentist and such. I have split her expenses with you, which I thought was fair.

Yeah, it was fair. Taking a deep breath, he walked up the sidewalk and onto the porch that wrapped around the side and front of the house. Damn, but it was colder than a well digger's...

He would have to watch his language around a five-year-old. The last couple of years had been spent with rough company. He had of necessity spoken their lingo. Now he could shut off that part of his life. It was over.

Just like his marriage.

The cost of serving justice had been high, but the safety of his family had come first, or else the price could have been even higher. The picture of a woman and two children, blasted beyond recognition by a shotgun, lingered in his mind like a horror movie. He'd arrived too late to save them.

Given a tiny twist of fate, that family could have been his. Dani and Sara. It was an image that haunted him in the depths of long, long, lonely nights.

A shiver snaked down his spine. He reached for the handle of the old-fashioned bell on the front door.

Danielle heard Sara's running steps cross the living room, the formal dining room that they used for a family room, and on the linoleum of the old-fashioned eat-in kitchen—the quaint, cozy kitchen being one of the reasons she'd bought the drafty old house that needed more repairs than a demolition derby junk heap. She laid the stirring spoon aside and knelt just as Sara rushed to her.

"There, darling, it's all right. Nothing is going to hurt you," she crooned.

She held her daughter tightly, every fiber of her being ready to fight or soothe or do whatever was necessary to protect her daughter from harm or fear or anything that bothered the five-year-old.

For a second she marveled at the ferocity of feelings that swamped her. She had rarely felt this intensity of emotion, not even in the heady weeks after meeting Kyle, not even during their first year of marriage when she had thought nothing could be more exciting than her dark-haired, blue-eyed FBI agent husband. Fear had put a different spin on the nature of her feelings for her child.

For a moment the loneliness and loss of something—perhaps her expectations that life would be good, that it would be fair—threatened her emotional control. This past month had come close to being too much—

Pushing the thought firmly behind her, she snuggled Sara close until the child's tremors subsided. Drawing back, she studied the frightened face of the five-year-old.

Blue eyes. Like her father's. Blond hair, thick like her own auburn curls, but wispy fine as children's hair often was and so hard to keep contained in barrettes or ponytail bands. At present, hair straggled over Sara's forehead and tear-reddened cheeks.

Fury crimped the corners of Danielle's soothing smile. If she ever got her hands on the men who had put fear into Sara's soul, replacing the trust and big-hearted goodness of childhood with the terror of being kidnapped and held for ransom someplace up in the mountains…

"Here, let's get you fixed up," she said lightly, putting a brightness she was far from feeling into her voice and smile. She, too, knew fear. Terror was no stranger to her heart. Her nights had been filled with it for weeks.

When her child had been kidnapped and forced to rely on her own quick thinking to escape, Danielle's view of the world had also changed. The two men who had taken her daughter, thinking she was Jenny McCallum, heiress to the Kincaid fortune, were still on the loose.

The police hadn't been able to find them after the men grabbed her daughter from the school parking lot. They hadn't been able to find them after Sara escaped from their lair, even though the authorities knew the general area where the men had held Sara because of the holly berries found in her hair.

December fourth to December eighteenth. Fourteen days of the most awful fear she'd ever known.

Then Dr. Winters had found her child running coat-less down the county road, her pixie face streaked with tears.

Anger seared down Danielle's spine like a hot poker. She hated those men for what they had done to her child. At times during the past month, she had hated the police for not preventing the abduction and for not finding her baby.

Sometimes she hated the FBI who hadn't answered her call for help after she had gotten Sara back and realized her child was still in mortal danger. Sara was the only one who could identify the men.

And Sara's father? Did she also hate the supercool FBI undercover agent who had deserted them, who hadn't answered her frantic calls for help?

She pressed her face into Sara's sweet baby flesh and fought a need to cry as loudly and painfully as her daughter. With an effort she pulled herself to-gether. There was no point in thinking about it. That was the painful past. She had the terrifying present to contend with now that she and Sara were on their own. They had been staying with Sterling and Jessica McCallum since Sara had been found. Sterling was a special investigator with the Sheriff's office and he had offered Danielle and Sara the protection of his home. Though Sara had enjoyed staying with the McCallums, who were the parents of her best friend, Jenny, Danielle knew her daughter needed to return to her normal home life sometime and so they'd come home after the New Year.

Taking a deep breath, she fixed the smile more firmly on her face. "Where's your pony band? Ah, here it is, dangling by a hair."

No answering smile appeared on Sara's trembling lips.

Danielle finger-combed the wisps of hair into place and replaced the band around the left ponytail, then did the same for the right side. "There."

Sara sniffed. She looked worried.

Danielle had consulted the pediatrician about the trauma and how to handle it, especially the fact that Sara hadn't spoken a word since she had been found. Studying her daughter, Danielle decided this wasn't a case of Sara's realizing she'd wandered into a room alone and rushing back to her mother or teacher.

Dear God, what more did she and young Sara have to face? How long could terror last?

"What is it? Can you tell me? What frightened you?" She spoke confidently. As if she could handle everything that life dishes out. Sometimes she wondered how close the breaking point was.

Sara stared at her mutely.

Danielle fought the anger and despair. "Show me, then. Did you see something? Or someone?"

Her heart lurched. She felt the reassuring weight of the semiautomatic pistol tucked into the back waistband of her jeans and covered by a flannel shirt worn over her T-shirt. She didn't know if she could aim it at a person and deliberately shoot him.

Do not give warning. Point and fire. Keep shooting until they stop coming.

The police training program played through her mind. If someone broke in the house, she was to go into the self-defense mode.

Assume they mean you harm. Because they do.

"Show me, love," she encouraged with a show of bravado. She would do whatever necessary to protect her child.

Taking Sara's hand, she gently urged her into the family room, then through the glass-paned doors into the big, drafty living room they never used in winter. Her eyes darted left and right as she tried to see everywhere at once. She didn't want to be surprised and not have time to use her gun.

Don't give warning.

The living room was empty of strangers as well as furniture. She couldn't afford to fill every room in the old house. "I don't see anything," she announced, the tension easing out of her neck and shoulders somewhat. "Perhaps you saw your shadow on the wall."

Sara shook her head vehemently. Curls escaped the hair bands and sprung out around her temples.

Danielle frowned as she checked her daughter's set face, her fear-filled eyes. "You have to tell me—"

The harsh *ring-ring-ring* of the old manual doorbell tore a gasp from her and froze the words in her throat.

She and Sara stood as if suspended in the shadowy world of late afternoon, caught on the cusp of winter's darkness and unable to return to the bright warm world of the kitchen where dinner bubbled in the pot.

The noise grated across her nerves as the bell rang again. Whoever it was, was impatient.

Still she hesitated. Would the kidnappers come to

the front door and ring the bell? Maybe pretending to be from the electric company or something? The lights had been flickering ominously all afternoon and a blizzard was churning up outside.

Sara tugged at her hand.

Danielle put on a brave smile and went to the door. She edged the window blind away from the etched glass panes of the oak door and peered outside, her heart going like a frenzied trip-hammer.

An unfamiliar shape stood in the dark shadows of the porch. Definitely masculine. Tall. Lean. His black Stetson wore a rim of snow on top and around the brim. His dark-blue parka was zipped up to his chin. She couldn't make out the details of his face.

Fear ate at her. Letting go of Sara, she put her right hand behind her and clasped the handle of the .38.

Point and fire.

"Yes?" she said into the crack between the blind and the etched panes. "Who is it?"

A voice from the past spoke to her. "Kyle."

It was shocking, like meeting someone you knew to be dead and buried right on the street, alive and walking. "Kyle?" she repeated as if she'd never heard of him.

"Your husband," came the dry reminder. "Open the door. It's damned...it's cold out here."

Sara peered up at her anxiously. For a second, Danielle could only stare at her daughter, her muscles locked in shock, anger, regret, too many emotions to name.

"Kyle," she said again. "It's your father," she said to the child. "Daddy. Do you remember?"

Sara, big-eyed with fear, shook her head.

Danielle pulled herself together. "Wait," she called out. "I'll unlock the door."

Her hand trembled as she flicked open the chain, the dead bolt and finally the old-fashioned key in the door lock. She turned the knob. A blast of cold air hit her in the face as the storm door opened and the man who claimed to be her husband stepped into the tiled foyer.

"It's colder here than in Denver," he said and took off his hat, then banged it against the door frame to knock the snow off onto the porch.

Danielle stepped back instinctively and felt Sara's warm presence as the girl hid behind her, one small fist holding on to Danielle's flannel shirttail.

Kyle removed his coat, checked the snow that clung to the shoulders and shook it off on the porch before closing both doors against the temperamental wind.

"Where can I hang this so it won't drip on the floor?" he asked while she locked up.

"In the mudroom." At his questioning glance, she added, "The kitchen. It's off the kitchen."

Trying to grab the tatters of her composure, she led the way back into the light. The homey aroma of beef stew calmed her somewhat when they entered the family room. She closed the French doors behind them to shut out the cold of the unheated areas.

Sara, Danielle noted, kept close to her and far from the silent man who followed at their heels. Looking over her shoulder, she encountered dark-blue eyes that had once turned her insides to jelly. An electrical current ran through her at the visual contact. She wasn't sure what it meant. The moment seemed surreal.

The bitter gall of subdued anger rose to choke her. It centered on the silent man behind her. She had needed him desperately and he hadn't come. With the memory came the silent, painful tears she never allowed herself to shed in front of her daughter.

"Did you get my letter?" she blurted, stopping in the middle of the kitchen. Sara scooted behind her and watched Kyle with a distrustful gaze.

He visibly stiffened. "Yes."

"Well?"

"We'll talk about it later. We have...other problems to deal with at the present."

He glanced pointedly at Sara, then back to her. So he knew about the kidnapping, she realized as he spotted the mudroom and went to hang his hat and coat in there.

Turning back to the kitchen, he silently perused her. She saw his gaze take in the thick socks she wore around the house, the jeans that fit her loosely after the ordeal of the past month, the flannel shirt that had once been his, an old T-shirt with an unreadable message.

She was aware she wore no makeup, that her hair, always unruly, was slipping from the rubber band at the base of her neck. She felt vulnerable, as if all her insecurities were laid out bare before the world. She didn't want him to see. He was a stranger, not the man she'd once trusted with all her heart. She'd lost that man, and she didn't even know how or why....

Aware of Sara watching them in her solemn way,

Danielle bit back the torrent of questions and strived for normalcy.

"We're about to have supper. Do you want to join us?" she asked.

Her innate politeness, taught at the knee of her loving parents, forced her to be courteous, but she didn't want to share anything with this man, this stranger back from the dead or wherever he'd been.

"Yes."

"Well, have a seat." She gestured vaguely.

He pulled out a kitchen chair and sat down with a weary sigh. "It's been a hell of...a heck of a trip."

"Two years." Her voice shook...with rage, with loneliness, with accusation. "You shouldn't have come. You didn't have to."

"You sent for me."

She denied it with a quick shake of her head.

His eyes narrowed. She watched him, tension in every nerve as if she might have to fight or run at any moment. His cheeks were dark with five-o'clock shadow and leaner than her image of him.

He was all muscle and bone and sinew. As sleek as an otter, every movement fluid and controlled. She remembered the way he could hold back until she was satisfied—

She cringed as if she'd touched a hot stove. She wanted to do something physical, like throw him out with her bare hands, to flail at him until all the pent-up feelings were drained and she was free of them. She wanted answers—why he'd deserted them, and why he'd come back.

But not now, not in front of Sara, who still trembled behind her, frightened of the man who had once been her favorite person.

Sara's father. Her husband. She wanted to cry.

"Dinner smells good," he said. "It's been a long time—" He broke off abruptly.

"Yes." Her voice was hardly above a whisper. She cleared it and spoke more firmly. "Yes, we'll eat. Then talk." She lifted Sara into her arms. "It's okay. This is…this is your daddy. Don't you remember him?"

The blue eyes darted to the man, back to her. Slowly Sara shook her head.

"She's frightened of strangers," she said to Kyle, leveling the blame at him with her gaze.

"I had to go," he said. "For you and Sara—"

"For us?" she interrupted in blatant disbelief. "For us you disappeared for two years? No visits, no calls, not even a note to tell us you were alive? This was for us?"

Sara hid her face against Danielle's shoulder. Danielle clamped her lips together, stopping the flood of questions and accusations.

"The case had reached a crisis point," Kyle said, his tone level and matter-of-fact compared to her emotional outburst, "Luke and the director agreed with my assessment that it was too dangerous for me to go home. You and Sara could have been at risk. I couldn't chance it."

"You and Luke and the director," she repeated with an effort to appear as calm as he did. "What choice was I given in the matter? When were my wishes and needs considered? Sara and I were whisked out of Denver in the dead of night without one word from you. Not one. So much for being a family, for discussing the future, for sharing decisions. So much for loving and honoring and cherishing.''

A flicker of emotion dashed through his eyes…Sara's eyes…then was gone. Guilt, regret, sadness? She turned away, angry and upset. He should feel guilty.

After placing Sara on the stool at the end of the counter, Danielle went to the stove. She dished up three bowls of stew, poured three glasses of milk and placed a wooden bowl of crackers on the table.

It seemed strange, setting dinner for three when for days, then weeks, then months, it had only been the two of them. She glanced at the dark-faced stranger at the table. For a second, she was more afraid of the man in her kitchen than the two men who threatened their lives.

Kyle inhaled deeply as Danielle set the stew in front of him. The aroma was intoxicating—the rich, meaty smell of the stew, the lemony trace of cleanser and wax used on the furniture, the scent that was unique to his wife—a blend of her cologne and powder and shampoo and her sweet womanly essence.

Home. But not welcome.

The knowledge dwelled in the bottomless pit that had taken over his soul. He studied Danielle's face, noting her carefully averted gaze, as she finished serving the meal and took her place at the opposite end of the table. Their daughter ate at the counter, still perched on the stool.

Silence fell over the room. An uneasy one. The

quiet that had first attracted him to Danielle was now a shield against him. She had withdrawn, enclosed herself in a cocoon of mute hostility that excluded him. He hadn't expected anything different after reading her letter.

But a man can dream. If only...

He buried the regret. Feelings didn't count in this case. He wasn't leaving until he found the guys who had kidnapped his daughter and now threatened his family. Then he would leave. If Dani said he must.

A tiny unexpected light flared in his heart. He extinguished it with an impatience new to him. She didn't want him here now. She wouldn't want him to stay.

"How long are you staying?" she asked, shaking him out of his introspection.

"However long it takes," he said.

Her frown indicated this wasn't an acceptable answer.

"I'm on R and R for two months." He figured he'd have the bad guys locked up by then. If not, he would stay longer. That was one thing she didn't have a choice about.

"Rest and recuperation," she interpreted. "Did you finish the case you were on?"

He nodded. Two years ago, he'd been assigned to a jury-tampering case that had quickly expanded into gangland violence involving extortion, gambling, racketeering, drugs, you name it. Upon seeing one of the gang's own family—the man's wife and kids—soon after they'd been blown to bits because of a disagreement with the gang boss, he had notified Luke, his contact at the regional FBI office, to get

Danielle and Sara out of town, just in case the crime lord should find out who he was and decide to do the same to his family. The deeper he'd gotten into their evil world, the more dangerous he had realized it would be for his family if he was exposed.

Her mouth tightened. "I can see you're not going to regale me with details."

Too late he realized he should have explained what had happened. But blabbing on about his cases wasn't part of his credo. It increased the chances of spilling too much to the wrong person at some unguarded moment. He had made it a habit not to discuss details at all. Life was simpler and safer...that way.

"The case is finished. Right now, I'm worried about you and Sara."

At the sound of her name, his daughter looked at him. Her eyes, so like his own, held fear and wariness. That distrustful gaze stabbed at something deep and primitive inside him.

A memory came to him. Sara, eyes sparkling, dashing into his arms as soon as he came home from a week-long chase after an escaped felon. The sweet baby scent of her—talc and lotion and grape lollipop.

A fist closed around his heart and squeezed hard. He had missed a lot of his little girl's life.

Danielle gave a little snort of ironic laughter. He looked a question her way.

"Yeah, it's a good thing we were here in White-horn where bad things never happen. When Luke said we had to go, I chose this area because my family once vacationed here. I thought it was safe."

He hadn't heard cynicism from her before. It bothered him that she had changed from his memories of her. She had been a friendly, unassuming woman when he'd met her. There had been a quietness about her. He had fallen into the enticing peace of her inner goodness and never wanted to come out.

Dani. Her name echoed through him, his talisman against the darker forces in his life.

He wanted to be buried inside her, exploring her passion, loving her gentle yet feisty ways, her flashes of humor. He needed her, the woman who had looked at him as if her world were contained in his arms.

The sense of loss hit depths that he had carefully avoided stirring for two years.

Danielle, unable to stand the long, empty silence during the meal, rose as soon as she finished. She excused Sara, who returned to a video she'd been watching in the family room, and took her dishes to the sink.

"Do you want more?" she asked, compelled to be polite to the blue-eyed stranger who had watched her with an unrelenting gaze the entire meal, his thoughts totally concealed behind the handsome planes of his face.

"Uh, no. Thanks." He brought his bowl and glass over.

She was at once aware of his warmth when he stopped beside her. He was over six feet tall and she felt his latent power as a threat to her peace of mind.

Why should she feel threatened by her own husband? Because he was a stranger. Because she didn't know what he thought about her request for a divorce. Because life was now filled with uncertainties on all fronts, and she didn't know how to deal with one, much less all of them at once.

Impatient with the jittery state of her nerves, she washed the few dishes, put them in the drainer and turned back to the room, moving a step away from Kyle.

"Oh," she said, feeling a cold dampness seep into her thick wool socks.

"The snow," he said, following her gaze to the wet tracks left by his hiking boots. There was a puddle of melting snow under the table, too. "I'm sorry."

"It doesn't matter. I'll get the mop—"

"It's my mess. I'll clean it up."

Without direction from her, he went to the mudroom and retrieved the mop stored there. He removed his boots and left them in the small room, then mopped up the puddles on the kitchen floor. He checked the family room and living room, cleaning up melted snow in there before returning the mop to its place.

"There," he said upon finishing. He glanced at her as if to see if she was pleased with his efforts.

It tore right down into her heart. Kyle's mother had died when he was young. His father was a stern, demanding man who had rarely praised him. She had found her husband endearing because he liked for her to notice when he did something especially nice for her.

She put a hand to her head, dizzy with sudden longing and wishing she could turn back the clock to the days when she had trusted him with her heart, when he had said he loved her...and then had shown her.

His gaze locked with hers. Questions thickened the air between them. And something more elemental.

She sensed the hidden hunger in him, could feel it ripple over her skin like a warm touch or a sigh. He was a man of driving passions, she had learned during their six years of marriage. Four years, she corrected. The last two didn't count.

Their courtship had been of the whirlwind variety. She, a quiet efficient librarian, had married a man she'd known only three weeks. Foolish people did foolish things.

Grimacing at the memory, she hurriedly gathered the rest of the dishes. Sara's stew was only half eaten. Neither she nor her child ate very much these days. Kyle had polished off every bit of the large serving she'd given him. For a second, she resented his ability to ignore problems when it came to satisfying his appetite.

She was probably being unfair. After all, he'd had no part in their recent terror. Frowning, she carried the remaining dishes to the sink. "So what did Luke tell you about us, about the kidnapping?"

She didn't lower her voice. Dr. Carey had thought it best to speak calmly about the event in front of Sara in hopes it would get her to open up about her ordeal. Other than being cold and frightened, the child hadn't been physically harmed, thank God.

"Not a lot. I want to hear about it from you. Every detail you remember. Also Sara."

"She doesn't speak. She hasn't since the kidnapping. Not once." It was another complication, one among many.

His head snapped around. He glanced toward the

family room where their child silently watched a video, then back at her. Danielle recognized the bleak pain that appeared in his eyes. It was a feeling she had learned to live with.

"Tell me about the men who took her," he said.

She was startled at his tone, harsh and businesslike. "Did the FBI assign you to the case?"

Another flicker of emotion dashed through his eyes. "You might say that."

Which was no answer at all. "Then you'll be staying until it's resolved?"

"Do you think I would leave you and Sara to face this alone?" he asked on a soft note.

A chill went up her arms. She'd heard him use that tone when he'd discussed a case with Luke by phone once. In it, she heard determination and grit and an absolute refusal to be distracted from ferreting out the truth.

"I don't know," she admitted.

A scowl darkened his face.

"How would I?" she defended herself. "You haven't been around in two years. You made us move away from the place we knew. You weren't here when we needed you—" Her throat closed and she couldn't continue. She held on and refused to give in to the despair. Who cared about a woman's tears?

"I know." His shoulder moved restlessly under the blue shirt that matched his eyes. "It will be different now."

Danielle swallowed a retort. Once she had accepted every word he told her as gospel truth. Once she hadn't minded his trips away from home. She had known he had important work to do that involved saving lives and righting wrongs. But those excuses no longer worked for her.

"You've changed," he said as if reading her mind.

"Two years is a long time." She headed for the family room. "It's time for Sara's bath. Tomorrow is a school day."

"It's a blizzard out there. You won't be able to drive to school," Kyle told her.

"The elementary school is only two blocks from here. We can walk. Besides, I have four-wheel drive on the car," she added defensively, feeling criticized.

"Did you get a new car?"

"Yes. From my savings."

With that parting shot, she left the room. In the bathroom, she started filling the tub while Sara went to their room and removed her clothing. The child brought back several bathtub toys and dumped them in the swirling water, then handed Danielle a book.

Danielle sat on the lid of the toilet to read while Sara acted out the story with her rubber bear and dog and doll family. "There once was a little girl with lovely golden curls and big blue eyes, just like you and Jenny," Danielle began the story. She paused when Kyle came to the door.

He gestured to indicate she should continue.

Sara shook her head. She pointed at the door and shook her head again.

"She doesn't want you in here," Danielle explained. "Men make her nervous nowadays."

"And I'm a stranger to her," he murmured.

She saw pain flicker through his eyes, an oddly desolate, lonely ache. She looked away. She didn't want to feel anything for him, not sympathy or need or desire, not anything. It was much too late.

He left without another word.

An hour later, Danielle returned to the kitchen. Kyle sat at the table. She saw he had made a pot of coffee.

She poured a cup and took her usual seat. Fatigue dragged at her heels. "There's a guest room upstairs. It isn't heated, though."

"Anything will do."

She pressed her fingers against her temples where a headache pounded with each heartbeat. "The attic bedroom will be freezing. The sofa in the family room makes into a queen-size bed. That might be better. I only heat part of the house in the winter," she added as if he had made some remark about her thrifty ways.

"The sofa will be fine."

His voice dropped to a deeper, huskier tone as he spoke. She remembered past homecomings, times when she had rushed into his arms, filled with the incredible excitement of his nearness, the demanding hunger riding high in both of them. They had been like kids in their eagerness to rush to the bedroom after Sara was safely tucked into bed.

"I share a room with Sara in the winter," she added for no reason. "I moved her bed in my room."

"There's no place for me in your bedroom," he interpreted. He gave a half smile. "I get the message, Danielle. I read it in your letter."

She was shaken by the incredible bleakness of his tone. "I just meant...I don't want any misunderstandings between us. At the end of your R and R, you'll leave."

He didn't answer, only stared at her until she looked away. She decided she'd been mistaken about the emotion.

"I'll show you where the sheets and blankets are." She rushed down the hallway to the linen closet and wondered who or what she was running from.

Chapter Two

Kyle woke instantly, alert and still. He heard the noise again. The coffeemaker burped, then began a rhythmic gurgling as it heated up. The radio came on. He relaxed.

The announcer detailed the day's weather. "Cloudy in the morning, perhaps some sun breaking through in the afternoon. Snow flurries again tonight. All roads are open at present. Schools will keep to a regular schedule until further notice."

Listening to his wife's quiet movements as she prepared breakfast, he faced the facts of his life. He was thirty-eight years old and he had blown the one perfect thing in his life. He would have to learn to live with that.

Some foolish part of him had hoped that Dani and Sara would rush to him last night and welcome him home. He pushed the thought down into the dark pool along with all his grief.

His own fault. Choices. Everyone made choices. Maybe his had been the wrong one....

He rose and pulled jeans and the blue shirt over his thermals, then padded down the hall to the bathroom. There was only one. He had discovered this after Dani and Sara had gone to bed.

He'd searched the whole house last night until he knew it like the back of his hand. In case of a nasty surprise by the kidnappers, he wanted to know every nook and cranny.

He had also chosen a room for himself across the hall from his wife and daughter. In the attic bedroom, he'd found a usable bed frame that he could move downstairs. The attic had been freezing, as Danielle had noted.

The old house could use a thick layer of insulation. And new windows, he added as the wind shook the panes and puffs of frigid air circulated around him. The foundation and framing were sturdy, but the place needed a major overhaul. It would cost a mint to hire the work done.

He had worked his way through college as a carpenter and was pretty good with his hands. But this wasn't his house. It wouldn't be his home. Danielle was right. He had left his family, no matter the reasons, and they no longer trusted him. He had no place in this house.

After a quick shower, he wrapped a towel around his waist and proceeded to shave.

Sensing a presence, he looked at the door. It was ajar and a small face peered at him through the crack.

He smiled and pushed the door open with his toe. "Sara. How's it going with you this morning?"

She ran off as if he had growled at her.

The fist squeezed his heart again. If he'd been at home the past two years, would his kid be afraid of him even after her ordeal? He knew the answer was no.

From deep inside, the pool of emotion he hadn't realized existed until he'd gotten that letter from Danielle shifted and churned bleakly. He finished shaving and went to the room where he'd stored his luggage.

Five minutes later he entered the kitchen. "Good morning," he said softly.

His wife spun about, fear on her face, determination in the set of her mouth. He watched her take in everything about the situation—him, the distance between them, the threat of danger. She was as edgy as a startled cat.

"Relax," he advised and pushed a smile on his face with an effort. "Okay if I have a cup of coffee?"

Danielle gestured with her left hand toward the pot. "Help yourself."

Her right hand, behind her and hidden by an old flannel shirt that he recognized as another of his, dropped to her side. She flexed her fingers as if they were stiff.

"I'm making oatmeal," she said, turning back to the stove. "Do you want some?"

"Please."

She nodded without looking at him and busied herself toasting English muffins and stirring a pot. A longing to go over and bury his face against the side of her neck, to breathe her fragrance into his starved body, speared right through him, churning up the dark pool. Regret rose to the surface. He would never have that right again.

"Sara, breakfast," she called.

He took a drink of coffee, studying his wife as she stood at the stove. The hot need that flooded his body took him by surprise. He fought the urge and conquered it. Control was important. It was all he'd had going for him many times in his life. It would get him through the present.

He had already accepted that his return wasn't going to result in conjugal bliss, so he'd thought he had the hunger under wraps. His libido was showing him otherwise. He carried the cup to the table and took a seat. His jeans were tight and uncomfortable.

"So, Sara, are you in third grade yet?" he asked his daughter when she entered and perched on her stool in thick pajamas that covered her from neck to toes.

She looked startled. Her glance darted toward her mother, but Danielle was busy elsewhere. Sara shook her head, slowly at first, then more firmly.

"Well, you're in first grade then," he teased.

This time she was a bit more self-assertive. She shook her head immediately.

"Oh, of course, you're still in Tiny Tots." He nodded as if remembering. "I used to drop you off at Miss Engles's on the days Mommy had to open the library early. We would have doughnuts for breakfast at the diner and keep it a secret because Mommy thought we should eat cereal."

"Sara is in kindergarten," Danielle interjected, bringing their bowls to the table. She frowned at him.

"Kindergarten?" he said as if amazed. "That old? You must be..." He pretended to search for an answer.

Finally Sara held up one hand, palm outward, fingers and thumb splayed. Relief eased the soreness inside. His daughter had responded to him.

"Five. That's right." He smiled in approval.

Sara stared at him with an unwavering gaze and no answering smile. Danielle served them without a word. She wasn't going to make this easy for him.

"Eat up," she said. "It's almost time to go."

She was speaking to Sara. He felt the chill of her rejection to his bones. *Please let me know your thoughts on the divorce as soon as possible,* her letter had read.

Always the polite librarian. But she was also his secret delight—his enchanting, passionate lover, the calm center of his being, all the good things in life.

The ache intensified. Maybe he should have handled things differently, but it had been easier to close off that side of his life than think about missing her and Sara. For their safety, he'd been willing to pay the price. He hadn't realized at the time it would include his soul.

Danielle forced her hands to move, to do the usual morning chores, to act normal when everything about her seemed so totally alien.

She'd spent a restless night—that was nothing new—but a new element had been added. She had listened to the sounds of Kyle prowling the house and wondered what he was thinking…feeling…if he was remembering…

Had he missed her at all during those two years? If he asked, she could tell about missing him and about the loneliness of being abandoned and wondering why. Why? she wondered again now. Because of the danger? He'd told her of that possibility before they were married. She'd accepted it and determined to live with it. He'd worked on other dangerous cases. There were other ways to protect agents' families without leaving them. She would have done anything to keep their family together. All he'd had to do was ask.

Shutting off the useless thoughts, she buried herself in the trivia of day-to-day living. "Shoes," she told Sara after the child was dressed in plaid flannel pants and a red turtleneck. "Hurry."

She put on her insulated boots and heavy coat after helping Sarah with her hat and mittens. They were ready to go. Kyle was at the door, dressed in the parka and black hat he'd worn last night.

"I'll take you in the truck," he said.

His tone indicated he was in no mood to argue. Giving him a hard look to let him know she would go because she thought it best, not because she was obeying his orders, she followed him to his pickup. She didn't want him doing things for them. She didn't want to learn to need him and then be deserted all over again.

Before she could do more than open the pickup door, he was there, scooping Sara up and depositing her on the seat, then his strong hands were at her waist and she found herself lifted as effortlessly as a doll and put firmly on the passenger seat.

"I could have gotten in by myself," she rebuked after he'd gotten in, put the truck in gear and backed carefully out of the drive. He gave her a glance and said nothing.

Her neighbor's son had plowed the drive before she'd gotten up that morning and the county road department had already done the street, so they arrived without mishap at the school. Danielle wasn't surprised when Kyle went in with her and checked the room out.

"Introduce me to the teacher," he requested.

Resentment flared in her, but she did as he ordered. Lynn was one of her best friends as well as Sara's teacher. "Lynn, this is Sara's father, Kyle Mitchell. Lynn Taylor, I mean, Garrison."

Laughing, Lynn stepped forward. "I was recently married," she explained, holding out her hand.

As Danielle watched the lovely blonde smile and talk to Kyle, a funny feeling came over her. Not that she was jealous. Kyle meant nothing to her. But she couldn't help remembering that once he'd brought her such joy.

However, she obviously meant nothing to him. A two-year absence without a letter or phone call proved that. She had accepted it, grieved over it and gotten on with life.

But she still felt funny watching him talk to her friend, even one recently wed and obviously in love with her very new husband. For a birthday present, she had given Lynn a makeover at the Whitehorn

Beauty Salon. The results had been startling as Lynn's natural beauty had surfaced.

Danielle, stifling the odd feelings, helped Sara with her coat and spoke to Jenny and her mother, Jessica. The girls ran to their table and took their seats, Jenny talking a mile a minute while Sara nodded or shook her head. Danielle's heart ached. She hoped their friendship lasted their whole lives—

"Sterling says there are no clues," Jessica told her and sighed resignedly. "We're afraid to let Jenny out of our sight for a minute."

"I know what you mean," Danielle commiserated.

"The Kincaid fortune," Jessica murmured, speaking of the legacy that had been left to her daughter when Wayne Kincaid and Clint Calloway, Jenny's half brothers, had given up their share of the Kincaid legacy. Both men had decided to put the estate in trust for Jenny. Neither man wanted anything their father, Jeremiah, had left them. Now Jessica understood why. "I agree with Wayne. The Kincaid name is nothing but a curse." After all, Jenny's life was in danger simply because those kidnappers knew what she had to inherit.

Wayne Kincaid had unexpectedly returned to Whitehorn after years of being away. Everyone had thought he had been killed in Vietnam, so the story went, but he returned under an assumed name to check out the town and the Kincaid ranch.

He had helped nab some men who were trying to destroy the ranch so they could buy it for a song, then, his identity exposed, he'd stayed on. He had married Carey Hall, the pediatrician who took care of Sara and Jenny. The couple had just been blessed with their first child together at Christmas, and seven-year-old Sophie, Carey's daughter from her first marriage, was delighted to have a baby brother.

"I didn't know your husband had returned," Jessica continued, looking over Danielle's shoulder.

"Yes, for a while. A couple of months," she added so that no one, including herself, would think it was a permanent arrangement.

Jessica cast her a quizzical glance but didn't ask any questions. Danielle was grateful.

She glanced across the room. The teacher was explaining the security in place for the girls to Kyle. Rafe Rawlings, who had recently been promoted to the town sheriff, had taken on the case himself and would be within a few feet of them at all times while they were at school. Lynn pointed out the window to a man dressed as a custodian.

"Sterling said Shane McBride was coming out to do a security check on your house this morning," Jessica continued after a thoughtful moment.

"Oh, good," Danielle said distractedly. Shane was the deputy sheriff and was working with Rafe on the case.

She felt she knew and had dealt with every law enforcement officer in the county during the past month. All except the one she'd needed so desperately—her husband.

Kyle strode toward her. "Ready?" he asked.

"Yes." She introduced him to Jessica. "Sterling McCallum is a special investigator with the sheriff's office—"

"I know who he is." Taking her arm, Kyle nodded to Jessica and ushered them out of the building.

On the way home, Danielle went over several opening statements in her mind and discarded them all. "Don't manhandle me in front of my friends," she finally said.

He cocked one dark eyebrow. "Only when we're alone? Okay, I can handle that."

She clenched her hand inside her mitten. "Don't touch me at all. And don't give me orders."

He turned in the drive and parked. Leaning against the door, he observed her for a long moment. "You ordered me out of the library the first time we met. It was time to close, but I wasn't finished researching old issues of the newspaper for information."

She stared out the window, wisps of memory floating around in her mind. It had been a day much like this one—cold and cloudy and threatening snow. She had ended up helping him, then walking across the street for coffee, which turned into a late meal, then he'd walked her to her car and driven behind her until she was safely in her small cozy house. He'd been waiting when the library opened the next morning. Her heart had quickened. When they'd married, he had moved from his sparse apartment to her two-bedroom cottage. Those had been the happy days, the star-crossed sun-kissed days.

"There's no point in remembering." She climbed out, slammed the pickup door and went into the house, her heart heavy with a mass of confused feelings.

He didn't come in until he'd made a circuit of the house and the stable in the back that had been converted into a four-car garage. After fighting a battle with her conscience, she had told him he could park there, too.

He'd accepted her offer and was gone a half hour. She figured he was checking out the building. When he returned, a cobweb caught on his hat confirmed her suspicion.

His dark-blue gaze met hers. She was at once aware of the silence that surrounded them. They were alone.

Flames ignited in the depths of his eyes. His gaze roamed over every inch of her as if he were comparing her to his memories the way she found herself constantly doing. Sweet, treacherous yearning blazed over her. Her body answered the question in his eyes with a resounding yes.

Shaken, she looked away. Her heart beat like a trapped bird in a cage. Once they would have rushed into each other's arms. Endless kisses would have been followed by endless caresses, the merging of their bodies and their souls. No! Don't even think it.

Stretching her arms to the side, she clutched the edge of the countertop and held on, waiting for her body to follow her mind's bidding. She gazed at the snow out the window and thought of cold things— winter rain, glaciers…loneliness. Heat radiated over her back.

Kyle's hands clasped the counter beside hers. His warmth caressed her arms, her back, her thighs. She was trapped. Like a cornered animal, she couldn't move, couldn't think—

"It's beautiful, isn't it?"

His cheek brushed her hair as he leaned his head near and peered out the window. A tremor raced through her.

"The mountains can help put life into perspective," he continued on a soft, husky note. "They lift our aspirations above the petty irritations of daily life."

She stared at the snow-covered peaks, but her thoughts didn't rise to lofty heights. They dwelt on more mundane matters—the earthly delights of kisses and lovemaking and the sharing of hearts and souls. She pressed her teeth into her lower lip and fought the yearning.

His hands touched hers, then glided up her arms. "When I look at the mountains, I think of you."

He caressed her shoulders, then slid his fingers into her hair and gathered it into bunches in his fists. Through their reflected images in the windowpane, she saw him bury his face in the thick strands and inhale deeply.

"Why?" she asked, needing to know more, seeking an answer to why he had left her. "Why think of me?"

He lifted his head and met her gaze in the reflection. "Because, like the mountains, you remind me of all the good things in life. You *are* the good things."

His gaze didn't waver, but compelled her to listen, to believe what he said. She wanted to. Heaven help her, but she wanted so desperately to turn and fling herself into his arms and beg him never to leave again.

"Dani," he whispered.

Her name seemed to echo through the silent house, full of need and a desperation she'd never heard from this man who had never truly needed anyone. His lips touched her temple. His hands gathered her hair and lifted it aside. He kissed the back of her neck.

She closed her eyes, feeling vulnerable and helpless. The way she had when Sara was taken. Helpless. And alone.

"No," she said. It was hardly a murmur.

"Don't shut me out."

She heard the agony, and it stunned her. The man she had known would never express such an emotion. He dipped his head. She felt the touch of his lips against her throat, a butterfly caress that threatened to melt the icy core that had enabled her to survive the past two years. For a moment, she imagined that he had been as lonely as she.

"No," she said again, stronger this time. "I can't go back. I'm not that person anymore." Whirling, she faced him. "I don't believe in us anymore."

Silence so deep, so filled with despair she thought she would weep, echoed around them. His features shifted slightly, becoming as unreadable as stone. He dropped his hands and stepped back.

She retreated to the small office off her bedroom and turned on the computer. Her hands shook. By sheer willpower, she forced her thoughts to the task at hand. She had a job to do. She had to support herself and Sara. She wouldn't depend on anyone else. She couldn't go back.

Bending her head over her notes, she began the task of checking actual library inventory against what the files said they were supposed to have. The inventory and updating of the files for the whole county library system had provided a much needed job and distraction from Kyle's disappearance when she had first arrived in Whitehorn. She worked twenty hours a week on a schedule that suited her.

She was building a life here. She didn't need anything else, or anyone other than her child.

A short while later Kyle appeared in the doorway. His face was devoid of expression other than the sternly disciplined remoteness he assumed when working on a case. "Rafe Rawlings and Shane McBride are here. You want to join us?"

She nodded, saved her data on the computer and followed him out to the kitchen. The two men were at the table, coffee mugs in hand. Kyle had made a fresh pot.

Make yourself at home. She sent the thought to her errant husband and couldn't decide if she was angry or not, or if she should be or not. A husband who wasn't a husband was a very confusing proposition. She avoided meeting his eyes. Therein lay danger, but she couldn't say what kind.

"Good morning, gentlemen. Please, keep your seats," she said, putting on her best hostess smile.

She flicked on the oven and prepared a pan of frozen cinnamon rolls, which would bake in ten minutes. She joined the men at the table in the meantime.

"Start at the beginning," Kyle requested of the men.

Shane McBride told Kyle about the day Angela had come to interview for a teacher's position and had been roughed up in the parking lot outside the school. Sara and Jenny had taken a shortcut through there on their way to rehearsal for the Christmas pageant and had witnessed the incident and started screaming. One of the men had chased after them and grabbed Sara, who, as the girls often did, had exchanged coats with Jenny McCallum. Jenny's name was sewn into her jacket and the two men believed they had the heiress to the Kincaid fortune.

"That's why they thought they could get a million dollars in ransom," Shane added.

"The McCallums got the money together to pay the ransom even though it wasn't their daughter," Danielle said. "I'll never forget that."

"No," Kyle agreed.

Their eyes met. They shared a second of complete accord that warmed some part of Danielle that had been cold for a long time. She looked away, remembering that her friends had been there for her while her husband had been working on the case that had demanded all his time and attention.

"Why were the kidnappers after the woman in the parking lot?" Kyle asked the detective.

"Well, it could have something to do with Angela's first husband. He was killed in an auto accident, but there were bad feelings between him and his partner, who disappeared after that. The business went bankrupt and Angela was left nearly penniless. And pregnant."

"Angela and Shane were recently wed," Danielle told Kyle. "Just before Christmas."

One dark eyebrow rose, but Kyle said nothing other than a congratulatory murmur to Shane, who nodded, a red tinge coming into his cheeks. Shane apparently had fallen hard and fast for the widow. Angela had had amnesia after the thugs had knocked her out. Upon recovering, she still hadn't been able to give the police any information. But Shane had taken her under his protection—and into his heart.

Danielle's eyes stung. Shane was gentle and protective with his wife. There had been a rash of marriages in Whitehorn recently. Dr. Winters, who had found Sara running down the road when she escaped, had married Leah Nighthawk shortly after the holidays. Lynn, Sara's kindergarten teacher and Danielle's good friend, had eloped with local attorney Ross Garrison after a whirlwind courtship.

Danielle brought her attention back to the discussion at hand. Kyle asked about the holly berries discovered in Sara's hair when she was found.

"We tried to trace her tracks but couldn't. The problem is, the hills where that particular holly grows are full of caves and old mining sites," Shane continued. "We looked over the general area."

"Did you take Sara there?" Kyle glanced at Danielle.

She shook her head. "Carey—she's Sara's pediatrician—didn't think we should. The trauma was too recent."

Kyle nodded, a dangerous expression in his eyes.

She realized he hated the men who had frightened their daughter as much as she did. If he ever got his hands on their hides, well, she could almost feel sorry for them.

Kyle sipped the coffee while he thought. "I'd like to explore the area myself. If you wouldn't mind." He glanced at Rafe, the senior lawman on the case.

Rafe nodded his agreement.

Shane spoke up. "You know who might be able to

help? Homer Gilmore. He knows these hills better than anyone. He's prospected them for years.''

"Where do I find him?" Kyle asked, sitting forward.

"That's hard to say. His daughter is married to a doctor here in town and manages his office. You could stop by and ask if she's seen Homer lately."

"I'll do that. What's the doctor's name?"

By the time the meeting broke up, Danielle felt they might be getting somewhere. Today was the first time anyone had mentioned the Gilmore person. After the two lawmen left, she turned to Kyle, excitement stirring inside so that she kept getting little odd pangs in her chest. "I want to go with you."

He gave her a puzzled stare. "Where?"

"To search the woods. Sara's pediatrician is married to Wayne Kincaid. They own part of the old Baxter ranch—"

Kyle held up a hand. "Slow down. What does the Baxter ranch have to do with anything?"

"It joins the Kincaid spread. That's where Sara was held, where the holly berries came from. She'd stuck twigs in her hair like she does when she played dress-up with her dolls. I want to help you look for clues."

"You used to do that," he said slowly.

"What?" She tried to think what she had done.

"Get excited about planning activities together. Your words would rush all over each other and your cheeks would glow. Like now."

He reached out and brushed his fingertips across her cheek. Heat rushed to the spot. His eyes darkened.

Memory and passion reawakened in her in an instant explosion of hunger and need. She had been alone so long, had been frightened and uncertain and helpless all the days Sara was gone. At times, while comforting Sara, she had longed for comforting, too.

She folded her arms and pulled herself inward where nothing could hurt her. "I needed you," she whispered. "I was so afraid. Our baby...our little girl. I didn't know if she was dead or alive. I didn't know if they had hurt her...if she was crying in pain...."

Tears filled her throat and she couldn't speak.

Arms enclosed her. His hands stroked her hair, and he spoke in a low soothing murmur. "I know."

For a second, she let the warmth flow around her, almost let it reach her heart. But this was fantasy and she had learned, oh, yes, she had learned, to deal with reality. She jerked away.

"You don't," she accused, her eyes burning, her chest hurting. "You weren't there. You didn't know. You didn't care—"

In one stride, he was in her face. "I cared," he uttered in a menacing snarl. "Don't ever say I didn't care. Because you don't know about that. You don't know what I had to give up—" He stopped abruptly.

She didn't flinch from the harsh stare. "What? What? Tell me. Did you spend scary nights in a strange town where you didn't know a soul? Did days go by while you waited for some word, for a call, a postcard, *anything,* that says the person you love is alive and remembers he has a family? And did worry give way to despair as you tried to answer a little girl's questions about her father and finally hear the child quit asking God to bless her daddy?"

"Dani," he whispered hoarsely.

She shook her head, the tears close, so close. "Did

you place frantic calls, only to be told nothing, except the person you needed with your whole heart and soul couldn't be reached, not even for an emergency? Let's compare notes. We can talk about the loneliness that tears the nights to shreds. We can discuss the fears that eat a person alive from the inside out. Then we'll consider what was given up and what was lost and what was thrown away—''

She choked on the words, unable to go on.

Not a muscle moved as he stared into her eyes. They stood as if frozen for all time.

Finally, a ripple passed over his face. "I can't,'' he said softly, sadly. "Talk is pointless. There's no going back, is there?'' He walked out of the kitchen, put on his coat and boots in the mudroom and left the house.

Part of her wanted to apologize. She wanted to wipe out the blackness that had permeated his gaze while he listened to the torrent of accusations. She wanted him to explain the sadness she had seen for a terrible second before he turned from her. She wanted to know if he really had suffered or if he'd just forgotten about them until it was convenient to come back.

She placed a hand against her chest and wondered if she was having a heart attack and if she wasn't, then how could the pain be so great. She thought again of the sad expression in his eyes. She sniffed twice and pulled herself together with an effort.

Maybe someone needed to invent a Richter scale to measure who suffered the most in marriage.

She couldn't find a laugh, not even a cynical one, anywhere inside her at the thought. Sighing shakily, she wondered why he hadn't explained or at least tried to defend himself during her tirade.

Because there was no defense for abandoning your family. It was a thing beyond understanding, beyond forgiving. But there was an answer: Because he hadn't cared enough to stay. If he had loved her…

She pressed both hands to her chest and waited for the ache to subside.

Chapter Three

Danielle frowned at the racket coming from the attic when she returned to the house after walking Sara to school the next day. What the heck was Kyle doing up there? She kicked off her boots in the mudroom and went to investigate.

She found him in the attic bedroom, dismantling the old brass bedstead in there. "What are you doing?"

"Taking the bed apart."

"I can see that," she stated impatiently. "Why?"

"I'm moving it downstairs to the bedroom across from you and Sara." He pushed a lock of dark hair off his forehead and straightened. "With your permission."

She wanted to say no just to be obstinate, but that would be petty. She nodded. "I'll help."

Gathering the six slats into a stack, she carried them downstairs and into the bedroom across the hall from hers. Kyle followed with the railings. Then she hefted the foot railings while he carried the headboard. Together they assembled the bed and aligned it against the wall.

"The mattress and springs aren't very good."

He nodded. "I thought I would pick up a set in town this morning. Is that okay with you?"

"For a two-month stay?"

"Sara will need something bigger soon. She'll outgrow the youth bed within another year."

"Yes. She's sprouting up so fast." Danielle started to tell him about how fast the girl outgrew her clothes. She closed her mouth on the words.

"What?" Kyle asked.

"Nothing. Just…she's growing…."

"I know." He took two steps closer. "Next thing we know she'll be putting on lipstick and heading off on her first date. And then to college."

Danielle tried to smile, but her lips trembled.

He reached over and ran a finger along her bottom lip. "Does that bother you?" He dropped his hand.

She shook her head, then changed her mind and nodded. "I want her to have a normal life, but I also want to protect her from ever getting hurt." She stopped, afraid she would reveal too much.

"The way you were hurt?"

Her gaze flew to his.

"Don't you think I know?" He shook his head. "I wanted to protect you and Sara from harm."

"Is that what you told yourself? That you were

doing it for our own good when you didn't contact us for two years?''

She thought of the nights when she lay in bed alone and wondered if he was dead or alive. She had agonized over him as much as she had during the fourteen days Sara had been missing. ''I don't think so. I think it was a convenient way to forget we existed. Your career was more important.''

Kyle grasped her shoulders and felt his wife steel herself, as if expecting him to do violence. It hit him—really hit him—his wife thought him capable of hurting her. He was a stranger to her as well as to his daughter.

After getting the letter, he knew he had lost his family, but he had never thought Danielle would distrust him, not his levelheaded Dani, who had matched his passion with her own, whose calm center had soothed his soul after his dealings with the harsh underbelly of society.

Her hazel green eyes continued to watch him warily. Her face was pale, the tiny freckles across her nose and cheeks visible as she waited for whatever he would do next.

''Two years ago,'' he said bitterly, ''I was assigned a case that seemed simple enough. The man I was after had no conscience. He would have gunned down his own mother if he'd thought she'd crossed him. If someone had followed me home or traced a call to you, if the gang had discovered I wasn't who I said, they would have wasted you and Sara without a thought. I couldn't take that chance.''

Her gaze didn't soften. ''You made a decision that

important to our marriage without consulting me. Do you think I have so little courage?''

She pulled away from his hands and bumped into the wall. The dull *clunk* he heard reminded him of something he'd noticed yesterday. He slipped his hand between her and the wall. The gun was tucked into her waistband. He pulled it out. A .38 semiautomatic.

''Are you licensed to carry concealed?'' he demanded, worry eating at him. Danielle was obviously determined to defend herself and Sara, but would she use the weapon if she needed to? It could mean the difference between life and death. With no idea how ruthless the criminal mind could be, she might think she could scare the kidnappers away.

''Are you going to report me if I'm not?''

She returned his glare without blinking. A standoff. His Dani was a match for any man. He smiled. ''I suppose I'm lucky I didn't get shot when I turned up on your doorstep in the middle of a blizzard.''

She retrieved her weapon and tucked it under her shirt once more. ''If Sara hadn't been present, I might have considered it.''

A tendril of auburn hair had escaped the band she wore around her head. He fought an urge to brush it off her forehead. Where his wife was concerned, he had forfeited all rights to them as a couple. He wondered if he had been wrong not to tell her of the danger and to let her make the decision regarding their safety. But it was too late for that. He'd done what he thought was right. Why did it suddenly feel as if it might be wrong?

''You were right,'' he said slowly. ''It was easier

to forget you and Sara existed than to think about you during the dark hours of the night. When this is over, I'll get out of your life forever, if that's the way it has to be.''

''How? You're Sara's father. Are you going to abandon her completely?''

''When did you develop that razor tongue?'' he asked quietly, then continued before she could come up with a retort, ''I'll expect visiting rights to Sara.''

He headed for the kitchen, needing to put distance between them and the desires that raged through him. Only Dani could make him lose control, and he couldn't afford that. He was pushed to the limit as need and futility knifed through him. He wished he could go back....

Danielle stared after him. The fact that he had offered any explanation at all on his absence stunned her. Why, she thought in frustration, couldn't he have explained himself two years ago? She would have accepted his decision for Sara's sake. But he hadn't even asked her. Maybe the danger had been a ready excuse because he'd been bored.

She went to her room to put on some lipstick and a pair of sneakers. ''I have to go to the library and do some work this morning,'' she told him, entering the kitchen a few minutes later.

''I'll drive you. I need to run some errands. How long do you think you will be?''

''Until noon. I thought I'd pick up Sara and stop for lunch before coming home.''

''I have some things to do in town. I'll go with you.''

The fake formality of the discussion bothered her.

"I don't need you to guard me. Sara is the one in danger."

"And you're a direct link to her."

"I hadn't looked at the situation in that light," she admitted. "The kidnappers could follow me...."

"Exactly. Ready?"

He led the way out the door, grabbing his parka as they left by the mudroom and went to the garage. The path had been shoveled.

"You've been busy this morning," she murmured.

He cast her an unreadable glance. His tone was cynical when he spoke. "As a long-term guest, I figured I may as well be useful."

A frisson swept down her back as she recalled times he had teased her about how useful a man was around the house. With that came other memories— long, lazy winter afternoons of football games and popcorn and lovemaking on the sofa in front of the fire, summer afternoons of hiking in the woods, of hidden meadows and a mossy bed.

Heat followed the chill, making her feel feverish and dizzy. She put a hand to her temple. Maybe she was coming down with something.

He stopped inside the garage and studied her. She couldn't meet his gaze. Last night she'd had such terrible dreams filled with danger and with longing....

"What are you thinking?" he asked.

She shook her head. "Nothing important."

His eyes darkened dangerously. "Then it must have been about me."

"It was about Sara," she lied. She was relieved when he climbed into the truck without challenging her.

On the way to the library, she berated herself for being susceptible to his masculine allure and the memories of their shared past. It was the sleeplessness, she decided, that made her restless and irritable and shattered her self-control.

Kyle went into the old brick building with her and inspected the place thoroughly before he left. She showed him the office where she would be working and gave her word that she wouldn't leave the building until he came for her.

Once absorbed in the inventory check, she set other problems aside. The hours flew past. The next thing she knew, he was back, standing in the doorway and watching her when she glanced up.

"It's time to pick up Sara," he said. "I would go by myself, but she doesn't trust me yet. I don't want to be alone with her until she does."

Danielle nodded and closed the computer files. She gathered her papers into their folder and tucked them into her briefcase. "Ready," she announced.

"I got the mattress and springs and took them to the house," he said.

"Fine."

He picked up her jacket and held it while she slipped it on. His fingers brushed her neck, leaving a trail of fire wherever they touched. She worried about that fact all the way to the school.

Rafe was waiting for them inside the schoolroom. "We had a report of two men spotted out on the county road near where Sara was held. The rancher said one guy was a stranger, but he thought the other was Willie Sparks—"

"Who's he?" Kyle broke in.

"A local boy, into misdemeanors as a kid, and some petty felonies—breaking and entering, shoplifting—later on."

"Do you think he was one of the kidnappers?"

Rafe shrugged. "I don't know." He glanced at Sara, who was helping Lynn put up the posters for class the next day. "I was wondering if we could show Sara a picture of Willie and see if she could identify him."

He and Kyle looked at Danielle.

"I would prefer to check with the doctor first and see what she thinks. It's only been a little over three weeks since Sara got away. She still doesn't speak."

Kyle's gaze locked with hers. "Sara won't be safe until we have those two guys behind bars."

"I know, but..."

"If we showed her several pictures and let her point to anyone she thought was familiar?" Rafe suggested. "We wouldn't press her about it."

Danielle could sense the men's desire to get on with the investigation. She resented the pressure they silently exerted. She pressed her fingertips to one temple where the beginnings of a headache pinged in her skull.

"Dani," Kyle said.

She jerked at the nickname. Heat flooded her body and rose to her face. The name had once been an endearment, spoken during the moments of bliss when his hands and mouth had roamed over her as they made mad, exquisite love and later, when they lay drowsy and content in each other's arms. *Go away,* she ordered the troubling memories.

"I...all right. But I want to be with her."

"Of course," Kyle agreed smoothly. "When can you arrange it?" he asked Rafe.

"Saturday?"

Again both men looked at her. Danielle nodded. "At the house. It will be best if Sara is in her own home. She'll be more comfortable than at the police station."

"Great. I'll come out around ten, if that's okay."

She agreed, then went to claim Sara. Rafe was gone when Lynn locked up and the four of them walked to the parking lot. After saying goodbye to the teacher, Kyle drove them to the main square in town and parked in front of the Hip Hop Café.

"This okay for lunch?" he asked.

Sara nodded before Danielle could speak. Looking at her daughter's pleased countenance, she agreed. She was sorry the minute they walked into the odd little restaurant with its mishmash of articles from ornate mirrors to a moth-eaten moose head on the wall. The town gossip sat at one of the tables. She motioned them over before Danielle could shepherd them in a different direction.

"Well, if this isn't a surprise," Lily Mae Wheeler exclaimed, her earrings, which were two bright-green parrots perched on gold wires, swinging madly from each ear as she looked from one person to the other.

Sara, who thought Lily Mae was neat, took a seat. That left Danielle no choice but to join them. Kyle sat next to her, his eyes busy taking in the dining room and each person in it. When he looked at her, he smiled.

Caught off guard, she smiled back.

"Well, so this is your husband," Lily Mae said.

"We've been wondering if you were real or made up to cover an embarrassing circumstance." She glanced meaningfully at Sara.

A dark red tinge crept up Kyle's neck. "Danielle and I have been married for six years," he informed the busybody in no uncertain terms.

Lily Mae giggled, then leaned close. "Well, years ago we had one librarian who told one whopper after another. Lexine Baxter left town as a teenager, then came back pretending to be a children's librarian. Turned out she was a criminal, killed her father-in-law and husband and no telling how many others to get her hands on the Kincaid fortune."

Danielle felt the air on her neck lift.

Kyle leaned forward. "Did she have a partner?"

"Oh, yes. She killed him, too. At her wedding to poor ol' Dugin Kincaid, would you believe?"

Kyle looked disappointed and settled back into the chair. The waitress came to take their order.

"I'm up for a chili dog with lots of fries on the side. How about you?" he asked Sara.

Her eyes sparkled and she nodded shyly. Danielle didn't argue with their choices, but, setting a good example, she ordered the vegetable plate lunch.

"Have you ever seen so many weddings?" Lily Mae asked when they were finished ordering. "Everybody's getting married on the run these days. Not a good thing, if you ask me. People should take time to get to know each other." She eyed Kyle. "What kind of work do you do? I might know of an opening you can check on."

"Thanks," he said, "but I don't need a job."

"Hmm, independently wealthy, huh?"

Danielle shifted impatiently at the woman's nosiness but said nothing. Kyle was an adult. He didn't need her help in fending off the inquisition.

"Seems odd that you haven't visited your family." Lily Mae turned to Danielle. "You and young Sara here have been in town about two years now, haven't you?"

"Yes," Danielle said.

Janie, their waitress, who also managed the place, brought plates of steaming food. "Lily Mae thought Wayne Kincaid was an escaped convict when he showed up in Whitehorn and wouldn't confess his life story to her. She had everyone thinking he was out to murder us in our beds."

Lily Mae glared at the saucy young woman. "Well, how was I to know? He acted as if he had dire secrets, not telling anyone where he came from or why he took a job at the Kincaid ranch when everyone knew it had a curse on it. And probably still does." Her heavily mascaraed eyes narrowed on Kyle. "It makes a body wonder is all."

Before thinking about what she was doing, Danielle snapped, "My husband's business is his own, but I can assure you he has no prison record. For your information, he's a good and honorable person. He works for the..." She noted the four pairs of eyes staring at her. "Well, he isn't a criminal," she concluded hotly.

"I'm with the FBI," Kyle said quietly.

"Well, the FBI," Lily Mae said, obviously flabbergasted at this piece of news. "Well, I never. The FBI."

Danielle clenched her hands together in her lap.

She was mortified by her outburst. A large hand closed over hers and squeezed gently. She glanced at Kyle. He withdrew his hand, but his eyes stayed on her.

His gaze roamed her face like a summer breeze, caressing her sweetly, conveying his thanks for her defense. The tension oozed out of her. She looked down, embarrassed but somehow glad...and maybe a little proud.

"Are you working on the kidnapping case?" Lily Mae demanded, recovering.

"I think that's in good hands," Kyle responded. "Shane McBride and Rafe Rawlings are on top of it. I'm home on an extended vacation."

Lily Mae's face lit up. "Rafe Rawlings. Now there's a story. Did you know he was called Wolf Boy because he was found in the woods when he was just a tadpole? Turns out he belonged to Lexine Baxter. Illegitimate, of course. She abandoned him, poor thing. But he was adopted by a local rancher, so it turned out all right in the end."

She continued the tale of how another rancher had been accused but acquitted of killing the man who had been Rafe's father. Turned out Lexine had done that, too, although that had probably been an accident. And then there was the case of Clint Calloway who, it was finally discovered, was the illegitimate son of that old scalawag, Jeremiah Kincaid.

Kyle frowned. "So how did Jenny McCallum get to be the Kincaid heir?"

"Oh, she was another of Jeremiah's bas..." Lily Mae glanced at Sara, who had lost interest in the grown-up talk and was busy loading her fries with ketchup. "She belonged to Jeremiah, too. Her mother died bringing the child to him. That's how come Jessica and Sterling adopted her. Lexine tried to get rid of Jenny, too."

"My heavens, she must have been the most terrible person in the world," Danielle said, shocked.

"Believe me, there are others just as bad," Kyle told her, his expression becoming harsh and forbidding.

"Like the case you were on?" she asked, reminded again of his long absence.

"Yes, like that."

Danielle was aware of Lily Mae hanging on their every word and glance. No telling what stories the woman would be spreading about them after lunch.

Not that it mattered, she reminded herself. This was but an interlude. Soon he would be gone again, out of her life forever. Except to visit Sara. When he had time. And that was the way she wanted it. It was.

Lily Mae regaled them with other stories after that. Danielle only half listened, but Kyle asked questions and wanted to know about everyone in town. He was looking for clues, she realized after a while, as he encouraged the town gossip to divulge more.

After the meal, Kyle drove Danielle and Sara to the grocery. Forcing a lightness he didn't feel, he and Sara joined forces to buy every treat in sight. Danielle kept saying no. She gave in to chocolate cake, though.

"Mommy always had a weakness for chocolate," he confided to Sara.

Sara gave a little giggle.

Danielle stopped dead in the aisle. Tears sprang into her eyes.

"What?" he asked, alarmed.

"It's Sara," she whispered, watching as the child scampered ahead of them. "She laughed. It's the first sound I've heard from her since she returned home."

"That's a good sign, isn't it?"

"Oh, yes!"

His heart contracted at the glow in her eyes. Once she had looked at him like that. Each time he came home, Dani had made him feel like a king. Suddenly he remembered something he wanted to do.

Clearing his throat, he said, "Thanks for defending me at the café. That was kind."

Her retort was keen as a blade. "One should always give the devil his due." She walked off, her chin high.

He had definitely been put in his place. But he'd seen her smile before she'd turned away. He smiled, too, as his chest eased a bit.

Danielle flitted around the kitchen, not doing very much but staying busy. It was Saturday and Rafe was due in a few minutes to show Sara the pictures.

"Relax," Kyle murmured from the table where he read the morning paper.

She glanced toward the family room where Sara watched a video. She spoke in a low voice. "I'm worried."

"About Sara?"

"Yes. Carey said to watch for signs of hysteria. If she can't handle the pictures, we aren't to press her."

He tucked a finger under her chin and lifted her troubled face to his. "I won't do anything to hurt

Sara," he promised. "All you have to do is say the word, understand?"

She nodded. Outside, she heard tires on the drive. "He's here." She went to the front door and let the lawman in. He carried a thick briefcase.

"I brought a bunch of shots taken this past year. "I thought we would show them to her in groups of six."

"Okay. Kyle is in the kitchen. We can work there at the table, if that's okay."

"Right," he replied, following her. "Hello, Sara, how you doing today?" he said jovially as they went through the family room. "You feel up to looking at some pictures for me?"

Sara looked at her mother, who nodded, then she nodded, too, and pointed to the television.

"As soon as her video is done," Danielle requested. "It has another few minutes. Come have a cup of coffee."

"That sounds good. It's colder out today than it's been all week. Too cold to snow."

"That's what Lily Mae told me a week ago…and then it snowed sixteen inches that night."

She and Rafe were laughing when they entered the kitchen. Kyle flashed her a quick glance, then welcomed the young sheriff. She poured coffee for them, then went to get Sara when she heard the end of the video.

Returning, she sat in her chair with Sara in her lap. Carey had thought that was best. Sara would feel safe and Danielle could tell if the pictures were upsetting her if she felt Sara trembling.

"Ready?" Rafe asked.

"Yes." Danielle gave Sara a hug. "We want you to look at some pictures and tell us if any of the people are—" She looked at Kyle, not sure how to describe the men.

"Sara, honey, we want to know if you recognize any of the men in the pictures," he put in smoothly. "If you think any of them are the ones who took you away. Understand?"

Danielle felt the tension enter Sara by the way she sat absolutely still.

"Do you understand, sweetheart?" she asked, stroking the baby-fine hair away from Sara's face. "You can point to the picture if you see one of the men, okay?"

Sara hesitated, looked from her to Kyle, then settled on Rafe.

"I think we're ready," Danielle said.

Rafe laid out six pictures, ranging from young boys to old men. "Any of these familiar?"

Sara looked at Danielle.

"Do you see either of the men who kidnapped you?"

Sara shook her head.

"Okay," Rafe said cheerfully. "We'll do some more."

They looked through picture after picture, six at a time. After thirty minutes, Danielle was getting tired. She sensed Sara was, too. "I think we'd better quit."

"We just have a few more," Rafe said.

Kyle touched her arm. "It's up to you and Sara."

"I suppose we can finish. If it's not too many."

Kyle talked to Sara while Rafe laid out the next row of snapshots. The pictures were the typical police mug shots. They would make Santa Claus look like a depraved maniac, they were so grim and unflattering.

"Sara," she said. "Look at these, honey."

Sara turned from her father to the table. She slowly looked at each photo. Then, she shook her head vehemently and put her hands over her mouth.

"She's getting tired," Kyle murmured.

"This is the last bunch." Rafe spread ten photos out.

"Do you see either of the men?" Kyle asked Sara.

Again she shook her head, both hands still clamped over her mouth.

"Honey, you didn't look," Kyle said patiently. "You have to look at the pictures to be sure."

Sara followed his finger and gazed at each mug shot. She shook her head.

"Okay, that's it." Rafe smiled at Sara, but he was clearly disappointed.

Danielle stood. "Come on, you can watch Frosty while Mommy and Daddy talk to the policeman."

Sara finally dropped her hands and nodded, obviously happy with the thought of watching two of her favorite videos in one day. Danielle saw her snuggled into the corner of the sofa and the movie on before she returned to the other room.

Rafe was ready to leave.

"Wait," she requested. Something in her tone must have alerted the men. "I think there was something about those last pictures, the ones where Sara covered her mouth and shook her head," she said in a low tone so Sara couldn't overhear. "I know Sara. She gets nervous when she lies. She'd been bored at that point, then suddenly she changed. She became tense and…maybe frightened.''

Rafe pulled out the last sixteen photos. The three of them looked them over. He pointed to one. ''That's Willie Sparks. Kidnapping and a million dollars is a pretty big operation for him, but with someone else directing, he could be in on it. I'd hoped she would pick him out so we would have something solid to go on.''

''I don't know,'' Danielle said slowly, troubled. ''I just don't know.''

Kyle laid a hand on her shoulder. ''Give it a rest for now. Maybe something new will come up soon. In the meantime,'' he said to Rafe, ''there's no reason we can't do some checking on this Sparks guy and see what he's been doing lately, is there?''

''My thoughts exactly.''

The two men exchanged grim smiles.

Danielle watched them with something akin to envy. They were comrades in arms. They spoke the same language even without words. She felt left out.

The loneliness of the past two years washed over her, reminding her she was the outsider. As soon as Kyle was sure Sara was safe, he would be off.

Chapter Four

Danielle put her hand over the phone and spoke to Kyle. "It's Jessica McCallum. She's inviting us to dinner tonight at her place. Shane McBride and his wife will be there. Do you think it's safe to go? Sara and I haven't been out at night since—"

"Not without me." He directed a level look her way.

"You're invited, too," she hastened to say, realizing she hadn't made it clear they were all expected. As if they were a real family.

"Yes. I want to talk to McBride's wife."

Danielle hoped Jessica hadn't heard his reason for attending. She spoke into the receiver. "Yes, we can make it. At seven? That will be fine. Yes. See you then."

Hanging up, she realized she had deferred matters

of their safety to Kyle. She shouldn't start depending on him again. He wouldn't be around long. A sigh worked its way out of her. A terrible heaviness settled around her heart.

Troubled, she finished flouring the chicken pieces she'd planned for supper, then stored them in the refrigerator. Finished, she stood at the sink, unsure what to do next.

Sara was taking a nap. The house was silent and forbidding. Danielle glanced outside the window, her gaze on the shadows under the pine trees as the afternoon sun slowly went down. As was her habit now, her eyes scanned the horizon, searching for the danger she sensed always around her and Sara. The feeling wouldn't go away!

"Relax," Kyle said, suddenly beside her. "You're as jumpy as a rabbit on opening day of the hunting season."

"I feel that way."

She tried to take a calming breath, but the scent of him caught in her throat. Once she'd loved to bury her face in the groove of his neck and shoulder and inhale the spiciness of his aftershave and the warmth of his skin.

Once, so very long ago.

The grief of his absence rose from that nameless place inside her, making her clench her teeth as pain pierced her soul and reminded her again of his leaving her.

A finger under her chin turned her to face him. "You look so forlorn sometimes," he murmured, his mouth no more than inches from hers. "Like an orphaned Bambi with no one to turn to."

"I've felt that way, too." She tried for a light tone, something to ease the tension that sprang between them.

"I'm not going to leave until this whole mess is cleared up. You have my word on it."

His voice was deep, solemn, a pledge to her and Sara's future. She fought an urge to lean into him, to share the burden of their child's safety, to admit all the many fears she'd faced during the past few weeks. She swallowed, then swallowed again as tears fought a battle with her pride.

"Because we're a case?" she finally asked.

"Because you're my family."

Their eyes locked, his hard and determined, almost angry. She knew the question had been cruel. "I'm sorry," she managed to say.

He shook his head. "It doesn't matter."

She heard the resignation in his tone, the knowledge that it was over between them. She saw the bitter despair in his eyes. She didn't understand it.

"You really cared about us, why would you stay away for two years?"

"I told you."

"Our safety." She shook her head. "A family stays together, works through the problems together."

"I made a decision based on the information I had at the time. I can't go back and change it."

He met her gaze steadily. Why did his being there make the death of their marriage seem so much harder? How could it have happened when she'd loved him so much?

"Dani," he said softly, suddenly, as if the old loving name were torn out of him.

For a moment, she saw the same torture in his eyes that she felt inside. She started to open her arms to him and offer him all the comfort she could give, knowing she would find the same in his arms.

The moment hung suspended between them like a golden thread of promise, tantalizing her with what could have been. Could have been, but wasn't.

"It's too late," she whispered.

He stepped back, his face once more controlled, an unreadable map of a place so remote she knew she would never find it. "Yes, I know." He gave an odd half laugh. "You don't have to worry. I won't force myself on you."

With that strange remark, he left her and went outside. Through the window she watched as he followed every track in the glistening snow as he surveyed her tiny kingdom. She had never worried about him forcing himself on her. That had never crossed her mind. She went to check on Sara, feeling like the doomed princess in some dark fairy tale that had no happy ending.

"There. That's it." Danielle pointed out the driveway leading to the McCallum house.

Kyle turned in. The headlights of the truck picked out the details of the vehicle already there. He parked behind Shane McBride's car. Sara unsnapped the seat belt and looked up expectantly, her eyes shining.

Danielle unfastened the belt and opened the door. Kyle took hers and Sara's hands as they walked up the snowy sidewalk to the front door. Jenny was there before they could ring the bell. "Come in," she urged.

She tugged Sara inside. Danielle and Kyle followed them as Jessica came to greet them.

"I'm so glad you could come. Kyle, it's nice to meet you again. Here, we'll hang your coats in the closet. There's a peg for your hat," she told Kyle.

In a couple of minutes, they filed into the living room while the girls scampered off to Jenny's room where her dog was banished for the evening.

Jessica introduced Kyle to Sterling—the two men had already met that week, Danielle learned—and to the other couple, Angela and Shane.

Angela, who was about five or six months pregnant, wore a holly-red maternity outfit with matching tights. Her cheeks were pink, and she looked healthy and happy. With her dark hair and green eyes, she was a perfect foil to Shane's clean-cut good looks. Shane was around Kyle's age, Danielle thought. Angela was in her late twenties, early thirties.

The two were clearly in love. It showed in the way they glanced at each other, in the way Shane's hands were there to help her up or hold her chair when they went to the dining room, in the way her tone changed each time she spoke directly to him.

Danielle's throat closed in the alarming way it did when Kyle had appeared on her doorstep, dusted with snow, during the blizzard. She followed Jessica into the kitchen where the girls were sitting down to their supper. Sugar, Jenny's dog, sat quietly by Jenny's chair.

"Sara wants a dog," Jenny told them. "She could ask Wayne if Freeway and Daisy have had any more pups."

Danielle noted the light in her daughter's eyes as

she gazed at Sugar and couldn't say no. "We'll see," she promised vaguely.

"A dog might be a good thing," Jessica suggested.

"It would bark at night if strangers tried to get into your house," Jenny said earnestly, her blue eyes solemn. "And it could bite the two bad men who took Sara." She squeezed her friend's arm. "A dog is a very good thing."

Sara nodded, then looked at her mother, her heart in her eyes.

Danielle sighed and gave in to fate. "I'll ask Mr. Kincaid next time I see him," she promised.

"I'll help you remember," Jenny said. "Wayne is my brother, just like Clint. I'll tell him if you forget."

Danielle couldn't help but laugh. "Thanks." She helped Jessica serve the crown roast and roasted potatoes. After taking her place at the table, she was startled when Kyle leaned close.

"You were laughing," he said. "That's the first time I've heard your laughter in two years."

She glanced into his eyes, then away. She couldn't face that heated gaze without melting, and she couldn't afford to do that. Kyle would be gone soon, back to his old life, the one he'd had before meeting her, she had realized during the long months of loneliness. The one he preferred.

"What was funny?" he persisted.

"I...nothing." Longing rose in her, along with the grief she thought she'd learned to live with.

"Jenny thinks Sara needs a dog," Jessica mentioned when she was through serving. "I think Freeway and Daisy have some pups that are about four months old. You should ask Wayne about them.

Sugar has been a wonderful pet. She's smart, a good watchdog and she adores Jennifer.''

"A mutual admiration pair,'' Sterling added. "It's very humbling to know you come in second to your child's dog in her affections.''

The six adults laughed. Shane patted Angela's tummy. "Maybe we should ask Kincaid about a dog for our girl here,'' he suggested, a world of warmth in his tone.

The tears rose perilously near the surface. Danielle fought to keep her smile in place.

"You know you're having a girl?'' Kyle asked.

"Yes. We saw her on the sonogram.''

Kyle frowned. "Did you have one of those?'' he asked, his deep-blue gaze on Danielle.

She nodded.

"Why didn't I know about it?''

"You were on a case, remember? It was the time you went to the Pentagon to talk to someone about the quasi-military group that had bought a place up in the mountains.''

"Did you know Sara was a girl?''

"Yes. I didn't want to, but I couldn't help looking while the doctor checked her out. She was sucking her thumb. I have a picture of it. I didn't show it to you when you got home because...''

"Because?'' he said, his voice dropping to a deep, quiet level that caused a hitch in her heartbeat.

"Well, I didn't think men were interested in things like that.''

"I think men are more interested than you women give us credit for,'' Shane told her. "We just have to be careful and act like we're not impressed, else you gals might think we're mushy and wimpy and all that.''

That drew another laugh. The conversation moved on to other topics like the town and the weather after that. Later, when everyone was relaxing over coffee in the living room, Sara came and sat in Danielle's lap. Jenny sat beside her father.

''I came here for the peace and quiet of the town,'' Angela said when Kyle asked about her coming to Whitehorn. ''Little did I know.'' She shook her head and glanced at Sara.

''The two men in the parking lot wanted to know about some money your…uh…late husband had?'' Kyle asked.

''They wanted to know where the money was. They said Tom had it and I had better hand it over. I can't imagine what they were talking about. The business was nearly broke, I discovered after his death. I don't know what he was mixed up in, but those men…well, they scared me.''

''You didn't recognize either of them?''

''No, they wore ski masks over their faces. They were dressed in jeans and winter coats. I have no idea who they were. Maybe I was a case of mistaken identity, too, the way Sara was because she was wearing Jennifer's coat.''

Shane took her hand when she sighed, her face puzzled and troubled by the strange happenings.

Danielle felt Sara stiffen slightly. Glancing down, she saw the child wasn't asleep as she'd thought, but was watching Angela, her blue eyes filled with fear. Danielle experienced once again the helplessness she'd felt upon learning Sara had been kidnapped.

Not even the gun in her purse—and yes, she was licensed to carry it—offered her any comfort. What chance did a lone woman and child stand against two hardened criminals?

Sometimes, usually late at night when she couldn't sleep, she doubted herself as a woman and a mother. Her husband had essentially abandoned her and their child, putting his case before their happiness. She couldn't seem to break through her daughter's fear and get her to talk. Maybe it would never happen.

Kyle laid his hand on her arm for a second, then moved on to Sara. The five-year-old's hand looked so tiny in his. She watched as Sara hesitated, then closed her fist around his thumb and held on, her manner slightly wary, but at the same time, trusting. She saw Kyle swallow hard and blink the sudden sheen from his eyes.

Her own smile trembled as she welcomed this first, tiny gesture of confidence toward a male that Sara had displayed since the kidnapping. Danielle turned her attention back to the conversation, which was still on the scuffle in the parking lot that occurred prior to the men grabbing Sara.

"I've wondered whether Tom's partner had anything to do with those men," Angela was saying. "He disappeared after Tom's accident, leaving me to straighten out the mess at the office and close the business down."

"What was his name?" Kyle asked.

"Dillon Pierce. I never liked him," Angela said, her nose wrinkling in distaste.

Sara pulled away from Kyle. She placed both hands over her mouth. Danielle looked on, puzzled, as Kyle watched their daughter intently. She leaned her head over so she could see Sara's face, but the child kept her head down and her hands over her mouth.

"Sara is tired. I think it's time we were getting home," Kyle announced suddenly. He stood and offered to take Sara, but she shook her head and buried her face in Danielle's neck.

Danielle saw the quick flash of pain in his eyes. "I'm sorry," she said. "It's just...it's not you personally," she finished lamely.

"I know. She's wary of strangers, all strangers."

His smile broke her heart. She looked away, feeling sad and confused and uncertain.

Danielle roused from her introspection when Kyle pulled up in front of the house. The lights spilling from the windows looked inviting...like home.

"Wait," Kyle said when he pulled into the garage and turned off the engine. He came around the truck and lifted the sleeping child from her arms.

Sara woke, looked from Kyle to her, then settled her head against his shoulder and went back to sleep. Danielle quickly went ahead and unlocked the kitchen door and held it open. Kyle carried Sara to the bedroom.

He watched while Danielle removed Sara's coat, then her clothing and slipped warm, footed pajamas on. She saw a smile dance at the corners of his mouth for a second before his expression became unreadable again.

"Let me," he murmured when she started to lift Sara.

He picked their daughter up and held her while

Danielle pulled the covers back on the youth bed. Sara opened her eyes when she was tucked in. She pointed to the books crammed into the headboard of her bed and gave Danielle an expectant look. A story was part of their bedtime ritual.

"It's late," Danielle told her. "You watched a video with Jenny—"

"I'll read her a story," Kyle volunteered.

There was a beat of silence while Sara looked at her father warily, then she nodded.

Danielle didn't have the heart to deny Kyle the moment with Sara. Besides, Sara needed to learn to trust some males again if she was ever to have a normal life. Nodding absently—she didn't want to make a big thing of it—Danielle busied herself around the room.

After Sara and Kyle had selected a book, he sat on the floor beside the low youth bed and began reading in his deep, pleasant voice. He liked to sing and had a fine singing voice, Danielle had discovered after their marriage, but he never used it in front of other people, only her.

When she had asked why, he shook his head and said nobody wanted to hear his caterwauling. Later, she had realized he was shy about it, except with her.

Her heart gave its usual hitch at memories of their former life together. She quickly gathered her nightgown and robe and went to the bathroom to change.

If only a person could excise the past from their brains as easily as a surgeon could cut out a defective organ, she mused as she washed her face and brushed her teeth. Finished, she drifted down the hall and stopped at the bedroom door.

Kyle finished the story and closed the book. He pulled the covers up around Sara's neck, then hesitated. Slowly, he reached down and touched her cheek with his lips.

Danielle held her breath.

Sara stared up at her father, their identical blue eyes only four inches apart. Then she wrapped her arms around his neck and planted a shy kiss on his jaw.

"Good night, punkin," he murmured, brushing a hand over the unruly curls spread over the pillow.

Danielle hurried away, down the hall and into the kitchen, her heart thumping for reasons of its own. He was a hard man in some ways. There was determination—maybe even ruthlessness—within him to do whatever he thought was right. But there was also that exquisite gentleness, a tenderness so true and deep it melted all sorrows and made the world right. Her world...he'd made her world right.

In a few minutes she heard his steps in the hall. When he came into the kitchen, she saw he had changed to blue sweats that enhanced the blue of his eyes and the sultry darkness of his hair. He was the handsomest man she had ever met, with a grace of movement in every line of his lean body. He smiled when he saw her watching him.

"Sara's foot pajamas reminded me of when we were first married. Remember how I told you there ought to be a disclosure law so that you have to tell the other person before you marry if your feet are going to be like two blocks of ice all winter?"

"Would you have refused to marry me if you'd known?" she demanded, falling into their former teasing ways without realizing.

"No," he said softly. "Nothing would have stopped me from that."

She managed a laugh, but wouldn't look at him. "My dad used to complain about the same thing. My mom told him it was a husband's job to warm his wife's feet."

Kyle didn't reply.

When she glanced at him, she saw his eyes roaming the lines of her fleecy robe. He paused at her slippers, which were really thick socks with soles. A smile appeared at the corners of his mouth, then flickered out. His face became still, but his eyes, oh, his eyes…

She turned from the despair she sensed inside him. She had grieved, too. Changing to a more neutral subject, she said, "I'm hungry. Would you like to join me for milk and cookies?"

"Yes." He moved away, over to the table. "You've lost weight. Was that recent?"

She brought the treat to the table. "Yes, after Sara was taken, I couldn't eat. I kept imagining her hungry and frightened. I didn't know if they were taking proper care of her."

He reached across the table and touched her arm. "It's okay now. She's going to be fine."

"Is she?" Danielle demanded, her anger rising as she recalled those terrifying fourteen days and nights when no one had been able to find her child.

"Yes, I think so. She let me read to her and tuck her in."

"She kissed you nighty-night," Danielle added. "You've only been here a week, but she seems to trust you."

"I'm her father," he said in a harder voice. "I was

part of her life for three years. She couldn't have forgotten me completely in the time I've been away."

Danielle ate a cookie, then picked up another. Many thoughts, accusations really, passed through her mind, but she didn't say them.

"Neither have you," he added softly.

The air became electrified. She couldn't breathe, or think. Gulping down the cookie with the help of the milk, she finished the snack and took her glass to the sink.

She gazed at the moonlight on the snowy lot next to the house. Across the way, the neighboring home was dark. The retired couple who lived there were already in bed.

Behind her, she was aware of every movement in the room. She knew when Kyle pushed back from the table, when he crossed the room, when he stood behind her. She moved aside.

He rinsed his glass and set it beside hers in the sink, then he turned toward her. His eyes gleamed dark-blue and mysterious as he watched her intently.

"It's time for bed," she said. "I mean, it's late. Sara will be up early. And we have to go to church."

"I know what you mean," he said. "You go to your bed and I go to mine. That's the rule, isn't it?"

She hesitated, then finding no hidden meanings in the statement, nodded briskly.

"You said in your letter that you wanted to get on with your life. Is there a man in your future? Have you met someone here?"

His eyes were burning her. She felt the sheen of moisture break out all over her body. His body heat engulfed her. She should move away.

"Is there?" His tone was harsher.

She shook her head.

"Has the cat got your tongue, too?" he asked softly.

Again she shook her head, then realized what she was doing. "No, of course not."

He traced a line down her cheek to the corner of her mouth. "You seem a trifle warm." His gaze lingered on her eyes, her lips. "So am I."

Her mouth went dry as longing seared through her—that terrible, terrible need to lean into him, to rest and refresh herself in the pure warmth of him. Once she had thought it endless, the great well of love they shared.

Tremors ran over her like cold rivulets of melting snow. "Go away," she said. "I don't want you here. I had accepted everything."

He dropped his hand to her shoulder. His thumb burned her skin where he rubbed it across her collarbone, even with the robe and gown between them.

"I need you," he murmured. "I did from the first moment we met. That scared me then. It scares me now."

She pushed his hand away. He curled it into her hair.

"You don't need anyone. Home…Sara and I…we were just a convenient place to stop between cases. A clean house, food, a warm bed—" She bit the words off too late.

"With a willing lover in it," he added.

"You could have found a woman. There were several at the office who would have welcomed you."

His fingers were sending tingles through her scalp

as he toyed with her unruly curls. His hand stilled as he studied her face. She refused to meet his gaze and stared out the window instead.

The snow, she thought, the deep cold snow. She and Kyle had married in winter. He had left them in winter.

And now the snow covered her heart. The only warmth inside her came from Sara. She drew a shaky breath.

"I never got mixed up with any woman," he said, almost as if musing aloud to himself. "I never meant to. But then I met you. All my good intentions fizzled with one look into those green eyes. There's never been anyone but you."

She couldn't believe him. She didn't dare. She had learned to live with the loneliness and the grief of rejection. She wouldn't go through that again.

"That can't be true," she protested in disbelief, her voice as shaky as she felt inside. "You can't have gone two years...you can't mean...there must have been women around. The molls—"

"The what?" He clasped her upper arms and leaned down slightly to peer into her eyes, his puzzled.

"Molls. The women that hang around gangsters."

Incredibly his face softened. He grinned. "Only a librarian would know some word like that. Molls."

He shook his head in amusement. Danielle was insulted by his attitude. She had imagined him in a variety of relationships during the past two years. She had even been afraid he'd left them for another woman, but Luke had told her rather impatiently when she'd called that Kyle was on an important case. She'd had to accept that explanation.

Gazing at her again, his smile died. "There's never been another woman in my life or in my bed from the moment I met you. Not one."

"Not even as part of your cover? Didn't the other men think you were a little odd?"

"I told them a woman had once betrayed me and that they were fools to trust any of them. I maintained that pose for two solid years."

Her heart went through a major contraction, then expanded until there wasn't room for it and lungs, too, in her chest. She couldn't breathe for a minute.

"Each time I was contemptuous of a woman," he continued, "I apologized to you. You were the most trustworthy person I'd ever met. The only one I've ever trusted completely."

She stared up at him, recognizing the despair in his eyes. It only made her more confused. She was unsure of him, of herself, of the old feelings that rose like a geyser inside her.

"Dani," he whispered.

He bent slightly and his mouth settled on hers, softly at first, like the kiss of a butterfly's wing, then more firmly when she didn't push him away. She sensed he held himself in check. Feeling the ripple that passed through his strong body, she knew the effort it was taking.

"Ah, Dani," he groaned and held her closer.

His arms slid around her, enclosing her in his warmth. She was instantly aware of his masculine strength, the pure male ruggedness of his trained body...and yes, the need.

An answering hunger clamored through her veins.

All week she had listened to his quiet footsteps in the house. She'd known when he went to bed, when he paced his room in restless agitation, when he paused outside her door before going to the kitchen.

He claimed her mouth once more, the kiss going deep and intimate, filling her starved spirit with the beauty of the moment and her body with a longing that couldn't be satisfied with only a kiss.

She knew she was on dangerous ground. She didn't want any regrets in the morning. She'd lived with a lifetime of those during the past two years. But she couldn't pull away.

Neither could she respond fully.

Kyle lifted his head. For a second, in the depths of his eyes, he seemed as emotionally ravaged as she felt. Despair, anger, need, physical hunger and the sadness…yes, the sadness. She knew the sadness on intimate levels.

"I want a place in yours and Sara's lives," he said, the storm passing and his expression opaque once more.

"For how long?" she asked.

His lips curled in a bitter smile. "It's always going to be there, isn't it? A gap of two years that I can't erase."

He walked out, leaving her standing there with a thousand questions that she couldn't ask, her body hot and bothered, her heart in shreds. All the things she had thought possible when she wrote her matter-of-fact letter detailing why they should get a divorce suddenly seemed impossible. She had no future with him. She couldn't imagine one without him.

She dropped her head forward and pressed her hands over her eyes, feeling as frightened as five-year-old Sara.

Chapter Five

"Rafe Rawlings available?" Kyle asked when someone finally answered the phone.

"Just a minute," the officer on the line said. "Hey, Rawlings, it's for you."

The door opened at that moment and Danielle entered the kitchen. She'd walked Sara to school that morning. As usual when he saw his wife, his heart clenched, then beat like mad for a moment before settling back down.

It was still pounding when the sheriff picked up and Kyle heard the click as the other man hung up.

"Mitchell here," he said. "I want to ask you a couple of questions that came up over the weekend."

"Shoot," Rafe said.

"Has anyone investigated a guy named Dillon

Pierce in relation to the attack and kidnapping in the parking lot?''

"Well, that was Angela Sheppard's...uh, McBride—she's married to Shane McBride now—"

"I know," Kyle broke in impatiently.

"Pierce was her first husband's partner," Rafe continued unperturbed. "Yeah, we did some checking on him but he'd left for parts unknown long before she moved to Whitehorn. There were no traces of the man to be found."

Kyle muttered an expletive. Glancing up, he noted the slightly shocked expression on Danielle's face as she lingered in the kitchen, listening to his end of the call. He had always been very careful about separating his home life from that of his work, especially watching his language in front of his wife and child. He felt a stab of guilt at the foul word but didn't apologize.

"Hmm, what about Willie Sparks? Any word on him?"

"Nah, he hasn't been seen in his usual digs, either, but that isn't unusual. He sometimes takes jobs at remote ranches or hauling logs for some of the small operators around the county."

"Okay, keep me posted, would you?"

"Sure thing."

Kyle hung up and turned toward Danielle. She was wearing a green sweater of that real soft material that reminded him of a bedspread, sort of like velvet. Her slacks were gray flannel wool and flowed over her hips in an alluring curve. She was in her socks. As usual.

Funny, the things he'd remembered while he was

away. Her cold feet. The socks. The little silky summer thing, the long gown for winter. The sweet sounds she made when they made love—all those soft, crooning notes of desire that had driven him wild.

Those things he'd given up. He had no right to the memories, either. They didn't help the situation. He'd done what he thought was right. He'd done it knowing he might never see her again. But he couldn't risk her life...

"Why are you interested in Dillon Pierce and Willie Sparks?" Danielle asked, breaking into the useless cross-examination of his past decisions.

He hesitated, wondering if he should mention what could amount to nothing. Seeing her stiffen, he realized he had offended her with his silence. Again.

"Never mind," she said and walked down the hall.

He followed, determined not to let the matter stand and fester between them. "I saw Sara's face when Dillon Pierce's name was mentioned. I thought I saw fear in her eyes, but she looked down, so I wasn't positive."

Danielle turned after flipping on the computer in her office. Her forehead crinkled into a frown as she thought. "I felt her stiffen when we started talking about the assault on Angela and the kidnapping. Then she put her hands over her mouth...."

Her voice trailed off. Kyle waited with the patience learned from years on the job.

"Was that when that man's name was mentioned? Dillon Pierce?" she asked. "Was that when you noticed she was frightened?"

"Yes."

"I thought so, too. It was just like when she was looking at the mug shots. I felt the jolt go through her whole body."

"Why didn't you tell me about that?" He subdued the impatience and gave her an eagle stare.

"I didn't think of it. Later, when we got home, I wondered if I should mention it to Rafe the next time I saw him. He was the one who showed us the mug shots."

"She covered her mouth then, too," he said. The pool of emotion shifted dangerously as she realized that Dani, his wife, hadn't thought to tell him, her husband and an FBI agent, of her suspicions. That told him better than words that she had no trust in him to solve the problem. Or to look out for her and their daughter. The bleakness rippled through him like the head winds of a storm.

"Yes," she said. "Yes. Kyle, there has to be a connection. There has to be!"

His heart skipped a couple of beats when she looked at him expectantly, her eyes shining like young Sara's. He looked away. He'd lost any rights to Dani when he had opted out of her life. But he could help her now. And he would. "Could they have been the two men in the parking lot?" Danielle voiced the question that loomed in his mind. "But how would the Pierce guy know Willie Sparks?"

"He could have followed Angela to town, then met up with Willie here. If Pierce didn't want Angela to recognize him, he would need a partner to help keep an eye on her."

"Wouldn't it have been difficult to find someone to work with him?"

"The bad types always find a kindred spirit."

She seemed to think about this for a moment, then was silent as she turned back to her computer, signed on the internet and downloaded a couple of E-mails.

When she was through, she turned to him once more. "How did you get involved with the gangsters? How do you know how to do it?"

His first impulse was to tell her nothing, but looking into those green eyes with their intelligence, with the new wariness of the human race that now resided there, he knew he couldn't gloss over the facts.

"You hook up with one of their minions in order to penetrate or you deliver some information they want, pretending you got it from someone in the pen, or better yet, from someone dead. You build up their trust."

She studied him for a moment, as if she was trying to see him—really see him—for the first time. Then her expression became shuttered once more and she bent her head over the keyboard. "I have to get to work," she murmured.

He bit back his desire to reach out to her—to make her look at *him* once more. Instead, he said, "Okay. I'm going to call Luke and ask him to do some checking on Dillon Pierce. Maybe he can come up with something on the guy. And on the business he was in with Angela's husband."

He didn't pick up the phone as soon as he went to the kitchen, though. He thought about trust and how it was built. And how it was destroyed.

As a child, he'd learned not to trust his father. After his mother's death, he hadn't trusted anyone very much.

Then he had met Dani.

It had all been so easy with her—to trust, to let himself dip deeply into the cup of life, to let her light shine in his soul. But she had learned not to trust him. She hadn't confided her observations about Sara to him. Just as he hadn't told her what he'd seen.

The darkness shifted inside him, making him aware of all the things he'd lost. His heart thumped painfully. He wondered if he'd been a fool.

Danielle hesitated outside Kyle's door. She wasn't sure if she should go in. But it was her house. And it was the day she washed the sheets.

Angry with herself, she flung open the door and froze in her tracks. Kyle was in there. Dressing. Or undressing. She wasn't sure which.

He wore a pair of dark-blue thermal pants and nothing else at the moment. They stretched over his body like skin, outlining every curve and muscle. Dark hair swirled over his chest and arrowed down to the thermals in a tantalizing line that drew the eyes to the bulge beneath the material.

As she watched, the bulge grew larger. Her breath caught in an audible gasp. She looked away.

"I thought you went outside," she said.

"I did. I stepped in a puddle that was iced over and went in up to my knee. I came back to change clothes."

"Oh." She glanced at the walls, at the neatly made bed, at his two pieces of luggage open on the floor under the window that had no curtain or shade to block the light. She looked at everything but him.

"Do you need me for something?"

"No. I was going to wash the sheets." She backed up. "It can wait." She closed the door.

In the mudroom, she threw the rest of the sheets into the washing machine and started it. Her heart was still pounding as if she'd run a long, long way.

Hunger riffled through her. She clenched her teeth on her lip and fought for control. This wouldn't do. Not at all. Not in any way. She wouldn't want him. She wouldn't need him. Not again. Never again.

Danielle held up the picture while Lynn clipped it to a line running across the top of the chalkboard. "Is that straight?" the teacher asked.

She and Danielle looked over their shoulders. Kyle studied the prints of the presidents who had birthdays in February. "Yeah, that's fine."

Lynn was planning a joint Valentine and presidential birthday celebration for the next month. She tried to tie learning to fun things so the kids would associate pleasure with knowledge. Danielle liked that idea, too.

Outside, Sara and a little boy whose mom was helping in the first-grade class played on the jungle gym. Rafe was on a ladder nearby, cleaning leaves out of a gutter.

She grinned and wondered if he resented doing such chores in his undercover pose as a janitor. She started to ask Kyle, then stopped. He had never talked about his work to her. He'd made it plain that part of his life wasn't her concern. She sighed and dismissed the spurt of resentment she felt whenever she thought of the past.

Hearing laughter, she went over to the window.

Sara hung upside down on a bar by her knees, her coat flopped down over her face. "Sara's laughing," she said to Kyle, needing to share the moment with him.

He strode over and stood beside her. They watched their daughter quickly climb off the bar and begin to chase the first grader. Danielle's shoulder brushed his chest occasionally as they observed the youngsters.

"Can't catch me," the boy repeated in a singsong.

Sara gave up running after him. She formed a snowball instead and zeroed in on the boy, hitting him in the back and splashing snow down his neck. A brief snowball fight ensued, with Sara, although smaller, giving as good as she got. In fact, her aim was better and she got in more hits.

"She has the eye," Kyle murmured in satisfaction.

"She should," Danielle countered wryly. "You started her playing ball as soon as she could sit up alone."

They smiled at each other. His head dipped. She thought he was going to kiss her right there in the kindergarten room. Lynn had her back turned to them. Rafe and the children were busy with their own thing. Without further thought, she lifted her face. Her lips shaped themselves for the touch of his.

He reached up and brushed at her bangs. "There. You had a piece of lint on your hair." He stepped back, his eyes darkly mysterious as he watched her.

She rushed off to see if there was anything else she could do for Lynn, her movements jerky, her face on fire. She didn't look back in case he was laughing at her.

They went to the grocery to pick up supplies after

she and Lynn finished. A storm was predicted over the weekend. She didn't want to get snowed in and run out of staples. She glanced at Kyle, who was maneuvering through the usual Friday traffic in town as people cashed payroll checks and did their shopping or went out to dinner.

"How about a pizza?" he suggested when they stopped at the store. "There's a pizza place right across the street."

Sara nodded vigorously.

"It's one of the four food groups, isn't it?" Danielle asked with a smile at her daughter. "Yes, let's have one."

"I thought Sara and I could pick it up while you do the shopping. If that's all right."

Danielle quickly studied Sara's young face. The smile had disappeared and the girl appeared solemn. "Do you want to go with Daddy to get the pizza?" she asked brightly as if this was a decision the child was used to making.

Sara stared at Kyle, her face worried. In a completely natural way, he held out his hand to her. Danielle felt her heart dip in sympathy as the five-year-old transferred her gaze to his hand but made no move to accept his touch.

"Well, Sara can go with me," she began, but at that moment Sara slipped her hand into her father's and clasped his thumb tightly. "Of course it's fine if she goes with you," Danielle added quickly.

"We'll meet you at the truck," he said in a husky tone as he led his daughter away.

Danielle watched them go as she unhooked a cart from a stack and started into the store. Another milestone. Sara was slowly opening up again. Hope bloomed inside her heart. Her little girl was going to be all right. She knew it.

At the house, Kyle told humorous stories about his experiences in the snow and the first time he'd gone skiing. He was originally from the South and hadn't come west until the department had sent him there while on a case. He'd liked the mountains and had decided to stay.

"That's how come Mommy and I met," he concluded. "She tried to throw me out of the library because it was closing time. But I took one look at those pretty green eyes and knew I wasn't going to let her get away. I made up a story about how I was on an urgent case. She, being softhearted, helped me look up the information I needed. I had her under my spell before we said good-night."

He waggled his eyebrows in a sinister mode and twirled an imaginary mustache. Sara giggled.

"I believed you," Danielle informed them indignantly. "I have all these years. I thought you *were* working on an important case."

His smile was lambent. "Well, I was, but it could have waited a day or two. I had to make you think it was a rush job so you would stay and help me."

"Huh." She started clearing the table.

"Sara and I'll do the dishes tonight," he volunteered with a wink at their daughter.

Sara laughed out loud. Their dishes consisted of paper plates for the pizza slices and paper cups for the drinks.

"See that you do a good job," Danielle told them sternly and left them alone. Going to the family room and turning on the weather channel for a check on the snowstorm, she listened to Kyle's pleasant voice while he kept up a steady, one-sided conversation with Sara.

Having her father back in her life was making a difference in the child's recovery from the kidnapping. That was good. *She* wouldn't trust him, but it was okay for Sara to. Sara had never felt abandoned because she'd had her mother, so it was easier for the child to forgive.

Danielle was startled by the thought. She thought she'd forgiven Kyle long ago and had gotten over her grief. Maybe she'd been lying to herself this past year.

The storm came with a vengeance that night. It howled down from the Crazy Mountains and through the pine trees, dropping snow in a torrent of fury. Sometime during the night, Danielle woke and realized the room was icy.

She shivered as she climbed out of bed and pulled on her fleecy robe and socks. Just as she'd suspected—the furnace wasn't working. Its fuel was gas, but the controls were electric and controlled by a thermostat.

"Let's build a fire and move in the family room," Kyle suggested, appearing in the hallway. "It's going to be colder than a well digger's…ah, as all outdoors by morning. No telling when the electricity will be on."

"Yes. It was out a week last year due to heavy snow. Trees were down all over town."

She padded after him as he went to the family room and built a fire in the grate there. She sat on the rug in front of the fire while it caught. She'd wait until the room warmed up before bringing a sleeping bag in and moving Sara.

"Something I thought of one day this week," she said, recalling the day at the school.

"Yes?" He settled beside her. He had dressed in jeans, shirt and a blue Nordic print sweater. He wore socks with a pair of moccasins on his long, narrow feet.

"If Willie Sparks was in on the kidnapping, then he would know Rafe isn't a janitor if he saw him at school." She glanced worriedly at Kyle. "Are the police using Sara as a bait to catch the man?"

"She's the only lead," he responded in noncommittal tones. "She's the only one who can identify them, so it's logical to assume they will be after her. A policeman has been parked down the street every night since you got home."

"Oh." She glanced at the window. "I hope he's not on duty out there tonight."

"I told Sterling I could handle things on this end."

She nodded. Pulling her knees up, she hooked her arms around them and rocked back and forth. "Even with this happening, I like it here. I think Sara and I will stay."

"It's a decent town."

"Where do you think you'll be sent after...after all this is resolved." She waved a hand in a vague gesture. She didn't only refer to the case but to the future.

"After the divorce, you mean?" he asked on a lower note, like the deep-voiced warning of the bass violin in an opera when something bad is about to happen.

"Yes. You usually work out of Denver. Will you go back there?"

"No." He looked her in the eye. "I'll stay close to wherever you and Sara are. I'm going to be part of my daughter's life from now on."

Her doubts must have shown.

"I mean it, Dani," he said in a tone that was almost menacing. "There will never be another two years like this last one. I'll quit the force and get a job here."

Her heart started a sudden pounding. Could she stand seeing him in town all the time? What if he married? It would probably be someone she knew. A wave of heat rushed over her like a blast from a volcano.

She couldn't believe how jealous that thought made her!

"We need to do something about the windows in the house," he said after adding another couple of pieces of wood to the fire. "The wind blows the curtain straight out in some rooms."

"I know. But it takes money to replace them. Next year, when I have a full-time job at the middle school, I'll be able to afford it."

"I can do it."

She shook her head. "That wouldn't be right. I mean, you won't be living here. It's my house, bought in my name. You shouldn't put any money into it."

His jaw set stubbornly. His mouth thinned to a straight line. "In other words, don't encroach on your life." He stood. "I think the room is warm enough. I'll go get Sara."

Danielle hurried after him to get the sleeping bag.

He was angry with her, but she was angry, too. He couldn't just come in and take over her life, not after two years of silence.

The storm dropped twenty inches of snow in fourteen hours. Two more feet fell during the next three days. Kyle moved the new mattress to the family room. Danielle and Sara slept on it in thick sleeping bags zipped together. He slept on the sofa in another sleeping bag.

Danielle found the enforced closeness electrifying, frustrating and fraught with danger. The tension seemed to mount hourly. The only way to handle it was by ignoring each other as much as possible and using Sara as a shield.

They didn't see or talk to another soul. The electric power and the phone were on and off intermittently, mostly off. Snowplows roared down the street at odd intervals, throwing a white plume fifteen feet in the air as they tried to keep the streets clear. It was a hopeless task.

A pristine blanket of pure white was laid softly over the rough surface of the earth as the lawn, the driveway, the lot next door and the field behind them were buried under five feet of new snow.

On Wednesday night, Danielle was fed up with eating sandwiches, heating soup on a camping stove and playing board games with Sara and Kyle for entertainment.

"Going stir-crazy?" Kyle asked with an amused lift of his black eyebrows as she paced from window to window.

"No," she answered and gave him a scowl.

He laughed. So did Sara.

Danielle's heart softened. The sole attention of her parents for five days had made the child blossom. That she now trusted her father completely was evident. Danielle was grateful for that.

She sighed and wrapped her arms across her chest as a puff of icy air hit her from the ill-fitting window frame. She was going to replace some of the windows before next winter, she vowed. But the cold was the least of her problems. Living basically in two rooms with Kyle for nearly a week was the major one.

Every nerve in her body was aware of him. She knew when he slept, when he lay awake on the sofa, when he prowled the house like a restless bear woken from hibernation. When he paused and stared down at her at night, half his face in shadows, half limned by the firelight.

He knew when she eased out of bed and sat in front of the fire, her thoughts on happier times. He knew when she heated cocoa and took aspirin to ease the tension headaches that plagued her. He knew when once she had stood by the sofa and gazed at his sleeping form. He'd opened his eyes, and they had watched each other without speaking for the longest time....

She had developed a new respect for his seemingly endless patience. She understood this was part of what made him a good law enforcement officer, or Feeb, as she'd heard FBI agents referred to by the local police officers during the ordeal of the kidnapping.

He had played games and helped Sara build airplanes and boats from boxes and paper. They had challenged each other with paper clip tosses into a plastic tumbler or cards into his ten-gallon hat.

Kyle was a good father. When he was available, she reminded herself ruthlessly. He could take off any time and they might not see him again for weeks, months, years.

She laid her forehead against the cold pane. Her blood churned feverishly through her body. Her head hurt. This morning she'd woken with a sore throat. Just what she needed—a nasty cold to complicate things.

"Feel bad?" Kyle asked.

"Yes." She felt his warmth at her back. "I think I'm coming down with a cold."

"Why don't you try to nap? You didn't sleep well last night. Sara has already conked out."

She glanced into the room. Sara was asleep on the sofa, an afghan tucked around her. Her cheeks were rosy, and she looked the picture of health and happiness. Danielle felt her throat tighten. "She's beautiful, isn't she?"

"Yes," he murmured, his eyes on her. "She takes after her mother."

Danielle shook her head. "Those eyes are her dad's. But her hair comes from my side of the family." She smiled and felt her lips tremble.

His deeply drawn breath sighed over her as he exhaled. The barriers dropped, and she could see plain raw hunger in his gaze. She switched her gaze back out the window as tremors rushed through her. She understood the need, the burning inside, the longing to touch, to blend, to merge that aching despair into the sweet hunger of the flesh.

There would be bliss. For a few minutes, there would be bliss. And forgetfulness. Appeasement.

And then?

She shook her head slightly. She didn't know and she was afraid to find out. The emptiness afterward would be too devastating.

"Dani."

His breath touched the side of her neck. She shivered as desire spiraled anew through her. "No," she rasped.

The tension mounted. Heat gathered in those secret yearning places inside her. Moisture collected on her upper lip, between her breasts.

"I'm sorry," he said in a whisper. "For leaving without talking to you first. For the hurt...for everything."

She couldn't help but respond to the agony she heard. "It's all right. It doesn't matter now. I...I've gotten past all that."

Ten seconds slipped by. He stepped back, and she felt the loss of heat at once. She stifled an impulse to turn to him and snuggle into his embrace.

"What the hell?" he muttered.

He leaned against her as he pressed close to the window. There, nearly hidden next to the bushes that lined that side of the house, were footprints in the snow.

Someone had crept up to the house—it had to have been in the night as the prints were nearly filled in with newly fallen snow—and stood outside the family room window and peered in at them. Only the distance of the porch had separated the person from them.

Fear shook her from head to toe.

Chapter Six

Willie Sparks put another log in the ancient wood-burning stove. The miner's hut, left over from a minor gold and silver strike in the early part of the century, was hard to keep warm. It could have been worse, he supposed. At least the roof didn't leak.

He glanced out the window. The wind still howled, bowing over the trees and whistling in through every chink in the tiny shack.

Across the room, Dillon Pierce snored softly from the lower level of the bunk bed. He was wrapped in a sleeping bag that covered all but the top of his head.

Willie wished he'd never gotten mixed up in this mess. What had started out as reclaiming an easy million bucks from some stupid woman had changed into kidnapping—Dillon's idea, not his—and now, maybe more....

He wasn't sure what Dillon's plans were. He didn't want to know. He just wanted out. He wanted to go home to his shabby but warm apartment in Whitehorn instead of camping out in the old mining town here in the ridges and hollows of the Crazy Mountains.

The mountains reminded him of his predicament. The Crazies were part of the Beartooth range, which were part of the Rockies—one thing within another thing, which was within another. Dillon had said his partner had bilked him out of the million dollars. So the quest for a million had expanded into kidnapping to get another million and now might expand into murder, and it had all started because of money.

He cursed to himself. The stupid woman hadn't known anything about any money. Willie wasn't sure if it even existed. Maybe Dillon had dreamed the whole thing up. Hell, who knew?

He just wanted to go home. Or over to the Kincaid spread where a fellow could get a hot meal just by dropping in, didn't even have to work there. That's the way ranching was—a cowboy was welcome to a meal at any time.

But now, with this kidnapping and all, he was afraid to show his face in town. Sara could identify him. She was a smart kid. After she'd surprised them without their cover while they were outside the cabin talking, they had quit wearing the ski masks.

Dillon sneered at his worries, but a man could go to the pen for a long time for kidnapping. He didn't even want to think about anything else his partner might do.

Take last night. That crazy Dillon had made him drive to the Mitchell woman's place during the blizzard. Said the snow and wind would wipe out their tracks. They'd used a snowmobile, which Dillon had suddenly acquired—Willie hadn't asked how—to get close enough to walk to the house when they had reached the outskirts of town.

Willie poured another cup of coffee and wrapped his hands around the cup to warm them. Sara had been inside with her mother. A man had been there, too. That had made Dillon madder'n a spring rattler.

Cute kid, that Sara. They had played cards while sitting in the drafty old cabin and waiting for word on the money. Dillon had scared her pretty bad, though, threatening to kill her folks and all if she ever said their names. No call for that kind of business. Willie was glad she'd gotten away while the two of them were out in the woods trying to shoot a rabbit for dinner.

He cursed long and silently. He hadn't bargained for murder. No, sir, that hadn't been part of the deal. He wished he could go home or over to the Kincaid place....

"They used a snowmobile," Kyle reported, returning to the house after several hours of tramping through the snow. "They crossed the field behind the house on it. They had parked a pickup on the other road, down behind a boulder pile in the pine trees."

"Did they go anywhere but here?" Danielle asked. "No."

A heaviness settled in her soul. "Won't this ever be over?" she said aloud, not expecting an answer.

"Not until the kidnappers feel safe." He hung up

his coat and removed his boots before entering the kitchen.

"And they won't as long as they think Sara can identify them, according to Shane. Why can't they accept that they've failed and leave the area?"

"I don't know."

Danielle poured him a cup of hot coffee, then set about making sandwiches for their supper. The soup was already heated, thanks to the return of electricity about an hour ago. No telling how long it would be on.

She glanced at the clouds still lining the sky and wondered if more snow was coming. The weatherman said the worst of it was over, but what did he know?

From the family room came the sounds of Sara dancing with Barney and his gang. Danielle wished she could hear her daughter singing the way she used to. She wished she could turn time back to December and make all this fear and danger go away.

The reassuring hardness of the gun pushed against her back. She'd stopped wearing it all the time since Kyle had returned. Now she had it securely in her waistband again. She had noticed that he'd worn his gun and holster when he'd gone outside to check the footprints.

"Did you check with Shane to make sure the sheriff's department hadn't been out checking on us?"

"Yes. It wasn't the police."

He came and stood behind her as she faced the window and peered at the snowy landscape. A few more snow flurries had fallen during the day, but they had been light.

"The plows have just about cleared all the streets,"

Kyle said, breaking through her introspection. "We should be able to get to town in the morning for groceries. I'm going to check out windows at the hardware store. I want new ones in here and the kitchen. And in your bedroom."

"No—"

"This is for Sara," he said harshly. "I'm also going to put in some infrared motion detectors in the rooms we don't use. Just in case. Anyone could break the locks and get in these old windows easily. New ones will be more secure."

"I'll pay for the windows," she insisted, giving him a stubborn glare to let him know he wasn't totally in charge of her life and home.

His lips thinned, but he nodded.

Fear settled along her backbone like an alien presence, one she should be used to by now. "I hate those men," she whispered.

"Just those?" he inquired mockingly.

She dropped her gaze from his. "There have been times when I hated you, too," she admitted.

"I know." He shook his head slightly as if saying it didn't matter. "I won't let anyone hurt you and Sara," he promised, surprising her with the vow and the intensity in his tone.

"Except yourself?" she heard herself ask softly.

His eyes went dark, bleak. She wished she hadn't voiced the accusation.

"You'll always hate me for leaving, won't you?" he asked just as softly, so their voices didn't carry.

"I don't know. Until this mess is sorted out and Sara is safe again, I can't think beyond the next minute."

"Didn't it ever occur to you that maybe the reason I didn't come home was because seeing you, I might not have been able to let you go?" he demanded.

She shook her head, unable to believe that was the reason.

"When you get time, think on that," he suggested and stalked into the other room.

They spent a stilted evening, using Sara as a shield between them as they played one more round of Monopoly. Sara bought every property she landed on, the bank, that being her father, lending her the money if she didn't have it. She won hands down over the two mostly silent adults.

The next day dawned fair. The roads had been cleared of all but an inch of snow. At nine, after seeing Sara safely in school and Danielle ensconced in her office checking the seemingly endless inventory lists, Kyle went to the home improvement store down in Billings and picked up the four sets of triple-pane insulated windows from stock. He ordered enough to replace every window downstairs and put it all on the joint credit card he and Danielle shared.

Spotting the pink insulating fiberglass stacked to the ceiling in one corner, he also bought as many rolls as would fit in the pickup. When the insulation was piled higher than the cab of the truck and tied on securely—it looked like he was hauling a giant wad of cotton candy—he headed back to Whitehorn.

Passing the FBI field office, he stopped there and picked up the motion detectors he'd requested and talked to the guy in charge.

"I'm retiring at the end of the first quarter," the

district field agent told Kyle, giving him an assessing perusal. ''We could use a guy of your experience here. I could put in a word for you. Luke Mason said he would, too.''

''Sounds as if you and Luke have discussed it,'' Kyle stated, frowning over the fact that his business was being discussed without his knowledge.

''Don't get your tail to twitching,'' the older man advised. ''We're looking out for the agency. You just happen to be in the right spot at the right time. Think about it.''

''All right. Give me another month before you say anything.''

On the way home, he mulled over the offer. He would be close to Sara. And Dani. If she married someone else...

Hell, he might have to shoot the guy right between the eyes. He couldn't maintain the brittle smile that formed at the thought. It bit too deeply.

The deep pool of despair shifted restlessly within. He'd known he could lose her two years ago when he'd cut her out of his life, his conscience reminded him. So there was no need to feel sorry for himself that it had come to pass.

But seeing her every day also reminded him of all the things he'd given up so that she and Sara would be out of harm's way as far as his job was concerned.

The kidnapping had shown him a person couldn't always order life to suit himself, that things could happen totally outside his sphere of control. The fact that he'd given his family up and they had run into danger anyway seemed unfair.

The fates must have really had a belly laugh over

that one—him being so damned noble in dropping out of sight without a trace while they plotted against his big sacrifice by setting up a kidnapping.

Last night, watching clouds drift across the room, he'd thought of those months when they'd been apart. Then, too, he'd spent sleepless nights, watching the moon and thinking of Dani. She'd been the light that had guided his soul through that valley of dark evil.

He muttered a curse as a rabbit cut across the road, nearly invisible against the snow. He finished the drive home in a dire mood.

Danielle and Sara were baking cookies when he arrived. The house smelled wonderful, like cookies and lemon cleanser—Danielle had cleaned the house, he noted—and shampoo and the faint scent of cologne. His women were all fresh and spruced up. Beautiful, they were.

Hunger stirred. He ignored it. "Hey, ladies," he said lightly in greeting. "I need some help to bring in the stuff I got."

"Let me get this last batch out," Danielle told him.

She was dressed in stretchy black slacks and a sweater that stopped midthigh, showing off her gorgeous legs. The hunger more than stirred. It sat up and begged.

"Come on, Sara, I'll help you with your boots," he said and got out of the kitchen fast.

Thirty minutes later, the three of them had the windows and insulation sitting in the middle of the living room floor. He showed them how the motion detectors worked with a remote control device. He explained that he would set them at night when they went to bed. If they got up, they were to come to him so he could turn the machine off before the alarm sounded.

"They will also be on during the day when I'm out of the house." He gave Dani the code to turn off and reset the machine if she went into the hall. "Anyone who gets in the hallway will cut the beam and cause an alarm. Call the police if that happens. Sara, can you dial 911?"

She nodded.

He set off the alarm so they would know what it sounded like. Then he had Sara practice dialing the emergency number under several different scenarios in which the alarm sounded or strangers appeared in the house, whether the alarm went off or not. They explored the house for hiding places. It had several that were good.

Satisfied Dani and Sara both knew what to do, he went to work on the windows. By nightfall, he had one new window installed in the family room. His hands were aching from the cold when he finally went inside.

Danielle examined the window. "Wow, no gale blowing in around the edges."

"The frame is insulated and the windows are low-e-radiant panes. That will cut the loss of heat, too."

"Now that's technology. Good job," Danielle exclaimed.

Pride rushed over him in a wave of warmth at her praise. Dani had always been able to make him feel worth a million bucks even if he only had ten cents in his pocket. She didn't judge a man by his money. She required other traits—truth and integrity, loyalty....

His disappearance could have been seen as betrayal and abandonment by her, although he'd never meant it to be that way. Looking back, he knew he would still do the same to protect them from the crime boss. But maybe he would explain his reasons next time.

Next time? Yeah, right.

"I'll get the other windows installed in here to-morrow if the weather stays clear. Let's have a fire and warm this room up again," he suggested. "Then after dinner, I'm ready for a hot game of Go Fish. Anybody want to take me on?"

Sara nodded vigorously. Danielle smiled but didn't agree to join in. Later, she opened a book and read while he and Sara played cards. It didn't take a genius to know she had effectively closed him out.

Kyle surveyed the attic. A good job, if he did say so. He'd had enough insulation to put in a single layer over the entire space, plus enough extra to put another row around the perimeter of the eaves. He would get more and finish the second row next time he went to town. He had also filled between the joists of the up-stairs loft and bedrooms, so they should be warmer in the future, too.

When Sara got a bit older, she would probably like her own private quarters upstairs. With a bathroom installed, it would make a nice space for a kid.

Forgetting he was standing on a loose sheet of ply-wood, he spun on one foot. The plywood flew up as his weight shifted and he windmilled wildly before stepping back to catch himself. That was a serious mistake. His foot came down between the rafters and landed on the gypsum board of the ceiling...then went right on through into the room below. He dangled there, one leg out of sight, one hung over a rafter. He gingerly pulled himself up and peered down through the hole.

Danielle stood in the kitchen, staring up at him, her mouth agape. "Uh, are you all right?"

He grinned. "Sure. That's the way I always exit the attic. Quicker than stairs."

After another second, a smile grew on her face, then she started laughing. She clamped her hands across her stomach and bent over, then collapsed on the floor.

"It wasn't that funny," he called down.

With a wry grin, he went down to the kitchen to survey the damage. His daughter, her friend Jenny and Jessica McCallum stared at him with varying expressions of disbelief and suppressed amusement.

"I'll be able to patch it with no trouble," he assured his wife, who was still laughing like a hyena but trying valiantly to stop.

"When I saw your foot come through, then your whole leg," she began, then had to stop while she whooped again. "I didn't know whether to try to catch you—" another choked spat of cackling "—or run for my life." She managed to finish with only a snort or two breaking up the words.

The girls looked from one adult to another, uncertain about the situation. Jessica had turned her head, a hand over her mouth.

Kyle tried to give Danielle a severe frown, but it was hopeless. He looked at the hole. A chortle pushed past the frown. It became a chuckle. Then a guffaw.

Dani gave up holding back and joined in. So did

Jessica. The two girls stared at the hole, then at the adults in puzzlement. "Come on, let's go play Barbies," Jenny suggested, giving up on the parents.

For the rest of the evening, the kitchen rang with merriment each time he and Danielle glanced at the hole or caught the eye of the other. Sara, still puzzled about what was so funny—after all, a hole in the ceiling was a pretty serious offense—giggled, too. Kyle realized it had been a long time since he'd truly laughed. It felt right.

"Hey, I understand you're pretty handy around the house," Rafe remarked to Kyle with a grin. "I have some ceiling work that needs to be done—"

"You can't afford me," Kyle interjected.

"Too bad. Several of the guys in the department had wondered exactly what you Feebs do. We hadn't thought about home improvements, though, as a sideline. Did congress cut your budget again?"

Kyle had been hearing jokes since his arrival in town that morning. He'd done some research into Willie Sparks's past record and looked at his mug shots again so he would recognize the man if they ever met up.

He and Rafe were having lunch at the Hip Hop Café. Danielle, Sara and Lynn, the kindergarten teacher, were eating at another table and planning a shower for somebody who had or was planning on getting married. He wasn't sure on the latter point.

"Did you follow up on those tracks?" he asked.

The smile disappeared as Rafe nodded. "You were right. There were two men who unloaded the snowmobile from the back of a pickup. We followed the tracks to the main road, but the plow had come through and wiped the road clean.''

"It probably didn't matter," Kyle told him. "The traffic, with everyone needing to get to town after the storm, would have wiped them out anyway."

"Wish we knew for sure who they were."

"You talked to the apartment owner and other renters?"

"Yeah, early this week. No one remembered seeing Willie since before Christmas." He shook his head. "It probably doesn't mean anything. People are busy during the holidays, or they leave town to visit relatives. Willie has his rent paid up through the end of January. I don't have any concrete reason for a search, so I haven't asked for a warrant from the judge."

"Yeah, since Sara didn't definitely identify him. But someone in those mug shots frightened her."

Rafe exhaled sharply. "Something will give soon. They'll make a mistake, and then we'll have them. Hey, there's Winona Cobbs. Maybe she can help." He waved at a woman who had just come in.

"Who's Winona Cobbs?"

"She runs the Stop 'n Swap, a sort of glorified junkyard, out on Highway 17. She's a psychic."

Kyle snorted. "Great. Now we're going to consult the stars or tea leaves for clues."

Rafe's expression was serious. "You'd be surprised at how often Winona knows something is wrong before we do. She gets vibes or something like that. Never had them myself, so I'm not sure of the fine points."

The psychic was a short, plump gray-haired woman in her sixties, maybe seventies. Her hair was in a single braid at the back of her head. She wore a long skirt with an Indian print shirt and a man's heavy mackinaw jacket. A string of crystals hung around her neck. She looked like a leftover hippie as she made her way to their table.

"Pretty out this morning," she said, taking a seat before the men got halfway out of theirs. "You're the FBI agent," she continued, looking him over with a keen gaze. "Little Sara's father."

Kyle met her eyes and sensed she saw much more than he would have wished. For a second, he had a sensation of his soul laid bare. He shook his head slightly at the odd idea.

"You'll get the men, both of them," she stated. "Sara knows who they are and she's told you as much—"

"Sara doesn't speak," Kyle muttered, the bitterness of not being there to protect his daughter riding over his heart like a herd of wild ponies.

"There are other ways to communicate," the psychic murmured, "if we will but listen…and look."

He nodded, feeling chastised and unable to say why. Sara had reacted in fear twice, but the police couldn't arrest someone without real evidence. Besides, they didn't know where Willie Sparks and Dillon Pierce were. Or if they were in cahoots. Or anything else."

"You been getting vibes on this?" Rafe asked, leaning forward and speaking in a low confidential tone.

She smiled. "Sometimes a person just knows things without knowing how they know."

Rafe nodded as if this explained everything. Kyle

stifled impatience at the seriousness of their manner. He didn't need vibes. He needed to nab the men who threatened his family. He needed them in hand—

"It will happen," Winona told him just as if he'd voiced the thought aloud.

"What?" he asked harshly.

"What you were thinking." She ordered the plate lunch special when the waitress stopped by, bringing the woman a cup of tea without asking. "There are other desires of the heart," she added when the waitress left. "But you must solve the conflict inside before they will be given."

"Can you give that to me straight?" He didn't bother to hide the cynical edge.

"You can win your wife back, but you must be willing to share your heart with her." Winona gave him a level perusal.

He was floored at the blunt statement and embarrassed that he wanted to ask her more. He remembered Danielle's reluctance to let him into her home.

He tried to explain. "A person makes choices, for the best of reasons. Maybe they are or maybe they aren't, maybe there were other, better choices, but once the road is taken, there's no pathway back."

Rafe looked from one to the other, questions in his eyes, but he stayed silent.

Winona nodded. "It's hard," she agreed. "But the spark is still there, isn't it?"

Kyle shifted restlessly. Was she talking about sex? Yeah, there was a spark. Danielle felt it the same as he did. But she had made it clear she wasn't going to give in to passion, that she didn't consider it a start toward a new life together. He had given up his life with her—

"Don't let it go out," the psychic advised.

"How?"

Her smile was kind. "In any way you can. You start with the tools at hand…just like with home repairs." Her eyes twinkled as she added this last.

Kyle groaned. "No one is ever going to let me forget sticking my foot through the ceiling."

"It's a small town," she conceded. "Memory is long here. Your Danielle is making a place for herself. There will be an opening for a new FBI field agent soon."

How the heck, he wondered, had she known that?

"No vibes. I saw Shane McBride yesterday. He mentioned you would be a good man for the job when the other agent retires later on."

The door of the café opened again. This time it was Lily Mae Wheeler. She took one look around the place then homed in on their table.

"Looks like we got another guest," Rafe muttered. "Better keep anything you don't want known under your hat."

Kyle prepared for more ribbing about his remodeling expertise. The town gossip would have for sure heard about it if the psychic had.

"Well," Lily Mae said, pulling out a chair. "I understand you'll be the new district field agent for the FBI." Her heavily mascaraed eyes flew open when the other three laughed heartily at her announcement.

"It has been mentioned to me that he's retiring," was all Kyle would admit.

"I hope you do better at your job than you do in

the home improvement field,'' she teased, leaning close to him so that he got a whiff of her perfume. The snowflake crystals that dangled on gold chains from her earrings twinkled merrily at him.

''Those are gorgeous earrings,'' Winona interjected. ''Where did you get them? I might need a pair like that.''

Kyle made it through the meal with the stoic patience he'd learned from years of FBI work. He didn't miss the amused glances he got from some townsfolk and the speculative ones he got from others.

On the way home—no, not home, not for him—he mulled over Winona's odd advice. It was almost as if the woman really did know of his past and had advised him on the future. He glanced over at Danielle.

Her face was composed as she watched the passing scenery. The aura of peace that surrounded her reached out to him as it had the first moment they met. The sun reflected off the snow brilliantly, and she squinted slightly against the glare. To him, she was beautiful.

Not classically beautiful, or movie star glamorous—her mouth was a little wide, her chin was a little sharp, but her skin was porcelain fair and as smooth as Sara's and her eyes…her eyes let you right into her soul…

She was all the good things in life, the things he'd had to give up while he lived in the gutters of society.

But the spark was there. He wondered, if he pushed it, if she would respond, if she'd be able to hold herself back from the passion that could bloom like a desert of wild flowers after a storm. Her passion…

In accepting him as her lover, in taking him as her husband, she had healed something in him that had made him think he was unworthy of a woman's love. And he, for all the loneliness of a lifetime of yearning, he wouldn't, couldn't, settle for any other once he'd met her.

From the corner of his eye, he saw her lick her lips and shift in the seat. Heat kindled from some internal hearth and slowly spread out to his limbs. He'd thought he had to give her up, even if it meant for all time, but the psychic had said otherwise.

And he wanted her. He needed her warmth, the laughter they had shared over the ceiling, the kindness that was so much a part of her that she had never understood when he had tried to tell her how special she was.

Without her, he felt empty. Sometime during their years together, she had become necessary. Only she could wash the blackness from his soul when he returned from the hell he found on the streets and in other people.

She made him remember why he fought for justice. She healed the disillusionment of dealing with the underside of life and brought the shine back to his soul. What had he given her but worry and grief and an absence even she couldn't forgive?

She was his reason for living, but he had no right to her, none at all.

"It seems your skills around the house are known all around the town," she said when he turned into the driveway.

He glanced her way. She was smiling. There was genuine mirth in her eyes. ''I'd fall through a hundred ceilings just to hear you laugh again,'' he said without feeling the least bit sappy about it.

Chapter Seven

Danielle saved the data on the screen, then turned off the computer. She was through with that batch. She stretched and yawned before heading for the kitchen for a fresh cup of coffee. Monday, February first. Standing at the kitchen window, she wished with all her might that the beginning of the month might bring with it the beginning of the end of this nightmare she and Sara had been living in.

January had been filled with danger and complications that she hadn't had time to sort through and figure out. Now it was February, a new month—

What was that?

She leaned closer to the kitchen window and peered at the stand of evergreens that lined the driveway. Had she seen someone out there?

She watched intently for a few minutes, but saw

nothing more. Probably a deer. They came right into the yard to eat the flowers she planted. She and Sara loved watching them.

Nature. That was the difference between the city and a small town. Deer, squirrels, rabbits, even an occasional moose or, once, a bear, and another time, a bobcat, had all paraded through the area.

Her heart lurched as movement caught her eye. No, it was nothing, just snow falling in a great cloud from a couple of pine trees, probably dislodged by the wind or a bird, maybe. Cardinals and jay birds wintered here.

The telephone rang, startling her. "Hello?"

"Hey, Danielle, how's it going? This is Luke Mason. Is Kyle available?"

"He's outside. In the garage, actually," she corrected. "I'll run down and—"

"Don't bother. Just tell him to call me at the office when he gets back to the house, will you?"

"Of course."

After hanging up, she went to the mudroom and slipped on her insulated boots. Draping a fleece jacket over her blue sweats, she dashed out the back door toward the old stables. Kyle had said he would be there if she needed him. He was probably changing the oil in his truck or something.

She entered by the side door and stopped dead still, wary of a strange noise.

Blat. Blat. Blat-blat.

She eased around the pickup and stopped again.

Kyle was there. Dressed in the bottoms of navy-blue sweatpants. Wearing sparring gloves. Using a bale of hay strung from a rafter as a boxing bag. He shifted effortlessly on the balls of his feet, dancing lightly around the bale, hitting it in lightning punches, then a low left to the middle....

Her breath caught as she watched, spellbound by his masculine beauty. He had worked up a sweat. His face and arms and torso glistened with it. The muscles rippled under skin that was smooth and still tan from summer.

He had been outside without a shirt, in spite of her cautions about ultraviolet light—

She broke the thought. His welfare was not her concern. He would do as he wished...just as he always had.

The strange, helpless need to cry rushed over her as it had several times since his return. She didn't understand herself anymore. Past thinking, she took a step forward, the need to touch him stronger than any she had felt this past month. His flesh would be hot to her cold hands, his skin slippery to her palms as she caressed him. He would warm all the cold places inside her—

No.

"Kyle." Her voice quavered. She cleared it and spoke again, stronger this time. "Kyle."

He stopped punching. His gaze jerked to where she skulked in the protective shadow of the truck. She moved forward at the same time he did.

She came to a halt in the middle of the sparring area. He didn't stop until he stood no more than a step away from her. "What is it?" he asked, tossing the gloves aside.

His voice floated down into the center of her being and she remembered his singing to her once after they had made love. "Annie's Song." By John Denver. The information entered her consciousness in bits and pieces, as if her thinking had become disjointed and random.

Tears stung her eyes. Kyle had filled her senses and her life with passion and joy. It had been a long time since she had felt either.

"Dani?" he questioned.

"Uh, Luke Mason said to call him when you got back to the house. He didn't sound urgent."

"Okay. Thanks."

She nodded, but didn't, couldn't, move. His chest lifted in deep breaths from his recent workout. She watched a drop of perspiration wind its way down his chest until it was absorbed in the waistband of the sweatpants. Other drops were suspended in the thick patch of black curling hairs on his chest.

Opening her mouth, she took a careful breath. Then another. She sighed shakily. It came out in an audible swoosh of pain, longing, despair.

"Dani?"

She shook her head, but she wasn't sure if she was denying the hunger that ran through her or admitting the hopelessness she felt inside. Against all common sense, she reached out.

Laying her hand in the middle of his chest, she let his heat and moisture soak into her, felt it flow along her arm and down her chest and into the deep, dark hidden place where passion and need lurked, ready to ambush wisdom.

With an effort, she lifted her gaze and looked into his eyes, his blue-as-the-sea eyes, fathoms-deep eyes, hungry eyes....

With a moan and a curse, he closed the gap between them. As he wrapped his arms around her and crushed her against him, she was helpless to resist, although she knew she should.

She closed her eyes as their heat met, mingled and grew to an inferno. She heard the roar of it in her ears and knew she would be consumed by their fire. It didn't matter.

Lifting her arms, she clung to his broad shoulders, let herself touch and explore and caress. His hands did the same to her, sliding over her back, along her sides, under her sweatshirt and back up. The cold air of the garage caused her to shiver. He pulled her tighter into his embrace.

Against her abdomen, she felt him spring to life with a suddenness that shattered any reserves of caution she might have. She had forgotten how quickly he had always responded to the slightest overture from her.

A heady sense of satisfaction spread like warm syrup through her veins. They had always communicated on this level, her need matching his. Partners in this. Equals.

But not in everything.

She shut the disturbing thought out. This moment…she would take this moment and never mind tomorrow.

"Dani."

He breathed her name into her ear, then planted kisses along the side of her face until he reached her jaw. He followed it to her chin, her mouth.

The kiss was long and deep and intimate—tongue and lips and teeth, searching, probing, demanding. A tremor coursed over her. His arms tightened convulsively.

He lifted his head and glanced around. She murmured a protest, then rained kisses along his collarbone and down his chest. She teased his nipple with her lips and felt it contract into a small hard nub. The salty taste of his perspiration lingered on her tongue.

"Come," he said in a hoarse whisper.

He lifted her into his arms and carried her into an old stall that remained after the stable was converted to a garage. Bales of straw were stored there, covered with a piece of tarpaulin. The last owner had kept a horse....

He laid her on the rough bed and eased his body over hers, his legs nestled between her thighs. She gasped as heat seared through her. Her body became pliant, moist, ready for his complete touch.

His gaze locked with hers. He moved, sliding slowly, intently against her. Even through their clothing, curls of desire, like vapor off a boiling kettle, wafted upward from the hot center of her being. Feverish, she clung to him.

He kissed her again, all over her face and down her throat. His hand delved beneath her top and found her breast. She wore no bra. There was nothing to impede the touch of flesh on flesh. He explored and teased until her nipples ached and spirals of electricity darted off into the interstices between every atom of her body.

How could she have lived so long without this, she wondered as desperation washed over her. She needed him, all of him, in her. Now.

She moved impatiently beneath him, arching upward against his hard shaft.

"Easy, darling," he murmured, a slight smile settling at the corners of his mouth.

"I want you," she said, squeezing her eyes shut.

"If it's half as much as I want you, then you're hurting."

"I am. I ache…inside."

"Yes. Like that," he agreed.

But he made no move to come to her. His hands, roaming and stroking and exciting her beyond reason, moved over her as he kissed her again. He nestled their bodies into a joint union of passionate bliss, his body stroking intimately against hers, driving her higher and higher.

Her breath became labored. So did his. She matched his movements, rocking to the rhythm that he used to guide their passion. Her blood ran fast, hot. She gasped as desire raced out of control.

He caught both her hands and held them over her head, his face just above hers, his eyes on hers. His face was chiseled into that intense mask of passion she had once known so intimately. She pulled her hands free and slid them down his back and beneath the waistband of his sweats, wanting them out of the way.

"I don't have protection," he murmured. "Do I need it?"

The question forced her to think. With that came a return to reality. All the problems, outside and inside their marriage, came rushing back. They had to stop this madness. When she removed her hands, she saw the knowledge of her refusal enter his eyes.

"Please, let me go," she said.

Without a word, he rolled off her and laid his arm across his face. The cold encircled her at once. "I'm sorry. It's just that—"

"Go to the house," he said. "I'll be in...after a while."

His voice was so utterly bereft, as if he'd come a long way and all his effort had been for nothing. She wanted to comfort him, but how?

Confused by the torrent of emotions, she fled the old stables and ran to the house as if Satan himself were on her heels. A man stepped from behind the line of pine trees before she reached the back door. She didn't think, she just reacted. Throwing her hands defensively before her, she screamed at the top of her lungs.

Kyle tensed in every muscle in his body at Danielle's startled cry. He grabbed his gun from its holster and ran to the door. He burst out, going down to his knees, his gun raised, ready to fire at whatever danger presented itself.

Danielle rushed toward him. He stood in time for her to fling herself against him. "A man," she said. "Be careful."

"Where?" His eyes raked the yard but he saw nothing.

"In the trees."

He put her behind him. "Get inside the garage," he ordered. "I'll check it out."

At that moment a white shape moved, separating itself from the snow-clad trees. The person walked toward them. He was covered in snow and looked like the abominable snowman, come to life.

"Halt," Kyle called out. "FBI. Put your hands over your head and don't move."

The man shuffled to a stop. Kyle realized it was an old man with a beard down to his chest, bundled up to his chin in a parka that was too big and totally covered in snow. He held something in his right hand. It looked like a jacket.

"Toss the jacket to the side. Carefully."

The old man did so, then raised his hands above his head. He was visibly trembling, whether from age, cold or fright, Kyle didn't know. He walked forward cautiously, keeping the gun trained on the man.

"Who are you?" he demanded when he was close enough to get a good look at the man, who looked ancient.

"Homer Gilmore," the man said.

The name rang a bell, but Kyle couldn't place it. At any rate, it wasn't the name of one of the kidnappers, nor did the doddery old man appear to pose a threat.

"The prospector that Rafe mentioned," Danielle said right behind him.

Kyle frowned. She hadn't followed his orders worth a damn. He'd have something to say to her about that later on. "Okay," he said to the man, motioning toward the house with the muzzle of the gun, "let's go in and see if we can figure this out."

Homer pointed toward the jacket tossed in the snow. "That belongs to your daughter. I was bringing it back."

"Jenny's coat," Danielle said. "Sara was wearing it when she was taken."

"That's right." Homer nodded his head vigorously. Snow fell in a shower around him.

"Were you under the trees earlier?" Danielle asked, moving around Kyle and up the path to the house.

Kyle gritted his teeth. She was between him and his line of fire. She knew better—

"Come on in," she called out. "Here, let's brush this snow off. I thought you were some kind of apparition when I first saw you."

Homer chuckled. "I was waiting for you to come back to the house. Didn't figure you'd be at the stable long in this weather."

Danielle cast him a glance as a blush mounted her cheeks. Kyle suddenly recalled that he had no shirt or coat on and that the snow, higher than his sneakers, was freezing his ankles. The temperature was around twenty degrees, but there was no wind blowing, thank heavens.

"Yeah, let's get inside," he echoed. He picked up the jacket from where Homer had tossed it and followed the other two into the house.

Danielle brushed the old man off and hung up his coat and wool hunting hat with its padded ear flaps. Homer didn't look much more presentable in his regular clothing than he had covered in snow. He wore several layers that made him appear bulkier than his sunken cheeks and skinny fingers indicated. His gray hair was thin and scraggly and hung to his collar.

"You look like you could use a warm drink and something to eat. I have some rolls I'll just pop in the oven," Danielle said after tossing her fleece jacket on a peg. She pulled her boots off and set them in their usual corner of the mudroom.

Homer did the same before trailing after her into the kitchen. Kyle kicked off his sneakers and headed for the bathroom. He needed a shower before he interrogated the prospector about the coat.

When he returned to the kitchen, dressed and warm once more, Danielle was laughing and talking up a storm. Their guest was, too. Both stopped when he walked into the room.

Like he was some kind of predator who had landed in the chicken yard. He frowned in irritation. She was never at ease around him.

He picked up the small coat that Danielle had hung on the back of a chair. Inside, the name Jenny McCallum was clearly labeled, probably so it wouldn't get confused with the other kindergarten kids' coats at school.

"Where did you find this?" he asked, taking a seat at the table.

Danielle placed steaming mugs of coffee on the table. "At an old mining camp up in the hills," she answered. "He'll take us up there if you want to go."

Kyle nodded. "Can we get through the snow?"

"He says we can," Danielle said.

Kyle gave her a pointed glance that told her to let the old man answer for himself. Looking more closely, he realized he could see the imprint of his body on her sweatshirt. The material was darker where it had absorbed the sweat from his torso when he'd held her. Heat rushed through him as need surged anew.

He wished they'd completed what they had started in the garage, but he no longer knew if she was on birth control or not. He realized there were lots of things he no longer knew about his wife.

In the two years since he'd been away, Danielle had changed. She'd always been a spunky, independent woman, but she had never been openly wary or hostile or remote. Not with him.

For a second he allowed himself to remember how she always welcomed him home, whether she'd just seen him that morning or at noon or a month ago, with a smile that reached all the way down to those quiet depths inside her.

For him. All for him.

She had taken him into her life, her heart and her bed. He had given her nothing in comparison to the gift of her love. His love, his devotion, his faithfulness to her—these meant nothing compared to the danger he carried with him wherever he went because of his job.

She followed his gaze to her clothing. Her cheeks went pink again. Turning, she removed rolls from the oven and set them on a plate on the table. "Help yourself," she offered.

He noticed her hand trembled slightly when she sat and picked up her coffee cup. He was reminded of the situation at hand, the irony being that when she'd needed him the most, when their daughter had desperately needed him, he hadn't been available at all.

Homer helped himself to the treat. "Might be easier to get through with a snowmobile. The Kincaid ranch has a couple of 'em. Wayne lets me use one when they ain't using it."

"Did you see anyone at the cabin?"

"Two men. Waited until they left before going inside and finding the coat."

"You saw the men?" Kyle asked. This could be the break they'd been waiting for.

"Yep. Not their faces, though. It was too far away. I stayed in the trees while they cleared out."

"Cleared out?"

Homer nodded. "I'd say something spooked 'em. They packed up and left, took everything. I thought they might have left a can or two of beans—"

Kyle pushed back from his chair. "I'd like to get out there right away. They might have left some tracks we can follow."

"Maybe they've left the area for good," Danielle said. "Maybe they've given up on getting Sara—"

"We can't count on that," Kyle told her, hating to dash the hope in her eyes. He watched as it flickered and died.

He noticed the lines of strain around her eyes and mouth and knew she had been holding herself together by sheer willpower since this ordeal had begun. Noticing his perusal, she lifted her head and met his eyes.

Admiration grew in him. She wasn't about to fall apart. He smiled at her. After a second, she smiled back, only an upturn of the corners of her mouth, but a real smile.

"We'll get them if they're still around," he promised.

"Yeah, those are the same tracks as the vehicle left over by your house the other day," Rafe agreed.

Kyle and the lawman stood by the logging road that gave access to the old mining town. They didn't need the snowmobiles to get to the site. The road was passable.

Danielle and Homer watched them from inside the pickup and the lawman's cruiser, which was a four-wheel-drive SUV. Homer had ridden over with Rafe. Danielle had insisted on coming with him after arranging for Sara to go home with Jenny McCallum after school.

Kyle followed the SUV as they made their way along the old logging trail to the cabin where Homer had found the coat. He and Rafe inspected the cabin. They dusted for prints but didn't find any that could be used.

"Someone wiped the place down," Rafe concluded.

"Yeah. Why do you think they're hanging around?"

"I've wondered that myself."

"I'm thinking Dillon Pierce still wants the money he thinks Angela has. I talked to Luke Mason at the FBI office while we were waiting for you. He checked on some things for me. There was definitely about a million dollars embezzled from the company Angela's husband had with Pierce."

"So he hangs around, trying to figure out how to get the money?"

"But first he has to get rid of Sara so he can move around town, maybe get a job and establish credibility while he figures out what his partner or Angela did with the money. It may be hidden somewhere and Angela doesn't realize she has it. I think he's figured all those angles and intends to stay until he finds the million.''

A call outside drew their attention. They found Wayne Kincaid, rifle in hand, talking to Homer and Danielle. His dog nosed over and sniffed them out. Kyle patted the mutt's head and scratched his ears.

''You've found a friend for life,'' Wayne told him. ''Freeway never forgets a good ear scratching. Homer says the kidnappers holed up here with Sara?''

''Yeah.'' Kyle brought him up to date.

Danielle listened, then spoke when he finished. ''Homer says there's a cave near here, that they used it as a jail during mining days. He said aliens locked him in it, but everyone thinks it was Lexine Baxter.''

''Where is it?'' Kyle asked.

''I'll take you,'' Wayne volunteered. ''Here, Freeway.''

Danielle, the four men and the dog followed a snow-covered trail through the woods to a clearing. There a ridge of rock lifted upward at a forty-five-degree angle from the earth. The mouth of the cave, fitted with a rusty iron gate, yawned like a black hole into hell.

''The girl was there,'' Homer told them. ''Her footprints are inside, but not the men's. She must've hidden here when she ran away from the cabin.''

Rafe and Kyle asked them to wait while they examined the cave for evidence. In a few minutes, they returned.

''Sara or another child was inside,'' Kyle reported. ''She hid in the back behind a boulder pile.''

His mood was grim as he thought about how cold and scared she must have been. And how brave and quick thinking. She had stayed in the cave for a while, probably several hours, until the kidnappers had left. Then she must have followed their tire tracks out to the main road where the doctor had found her and brought her to town.

Thank God Jeremy Winters had happened by when he did. Kyle hated to think what might have happened if the kidnappers, or someone worse, had come upon her. A hand slid into his.

"It's okay," Danielle murmured. "She's okay."

"She doesn't talk," he reminded her.

"But she will. I'm sure of it."

Her smile smote his heart. *Dani.* Her name was the prayer he couldn't utter. He wished he could turn back the clock. If he'd been there, Sara might not have been taken. Maybe he would have gone by the school to pick her up and seen the two men attack the woman in the parking lot. He could have stopped them—

He shook his head. There was no going back. Danielle had succumbed momentarily to the passion between them, but she hadn't accepted him back in her life. He'd lost any right to even hope for it.

"Well, that's it," Rafe said, putting his flashlight in the police cruiser. "Now all we need to do is find out where they've holed up this time." He turned to the old man. "I appreciate your help in this, Homer. You want a ride back to your daughter's place?"

Homer nodded.

Danielle remembered to ask Wayne about a dog for Sara. He said he had a cute little female that needed a home. He'd bring it by one day soon and Sara could decide if it was the one for her.

They left Wayne and his dog at his truck on the Kincaid place, then drove into town. Rafe waved when Kyle turned off on Danielle's street.

"We're back to square one," she said and sighed.

"Don't be discouraged. We've got them on the run now. They'll leave tracks. And make a mistake."

She looked skeptical, but didn't argue as they went into the silent house. It was a mess.

"Someone broke in," she said.

Kyle noted her stunned look, but only had time to give her a comforting pat on the shoulder. He realized he hadn't set the motion detectors when they'd left the house with Homer. A mistake on his part. Damn.

Willie carried the last of the supplies inside and slammed the door with his foot. He dumped the stuff on the rickety table in the old snow shelter shack and grimaced.

Here he was—in another log cabin in the woods. At least it was in good repair. The forest service maintained it.

He'd had a devil of a time getting to the place. Dillon had ended up breaking a trail for the truck with the snowmobile. Even with that and using four-wheel drive, he'd had a hard time driving the pickup over the icy road.

He wished he'd never gotten involved in this mess.

Glumly, he straightened up the cabin and put the stuff they'd stolen from the kid's house in the cabinets along one wall. Dillon didn't help. He'd come in, started a fire in the stove that served for cooking and heating, then had settled himself in a chair and let Willie do all the work.

Damn, but he wished he'd taken that job at the Kincaid ranch. They always needed help. Some people thought the place had a curse on it. Hell, anything would be better than this mess with Dillon. When he'd said he was leaving, Dillon had threatened him...*him,* his partner in this fiasco.

Fine way to treat a man.

Over at the Kincaid place, they always treated their cowhands decent-like. Hot food. A warm bunkhouse. Television and a VCR. A good selection of movies. He'd always liked that one about the dog. *Old Yeller,* it was called. His eyes smarted. They'd had to shoot the beast at the end. He wouldn't have had the heart to do it.

Hell, he couldn't even shoot a rabbit. His dad had laughed at him....

Well, that was the old days. His old man was in the ground now, right where he deserved to be, drunken lout that he was. A wife and kid beater.

At least *he* had never hit a woman or kid, not in his whole life. Which was pretty miserable right now. He cast Dillon a resentful glance, but the baboon didn't notice. All Dillon thought about was getting that million dollars. If there was a million dollars. Which he doubted.

He wolfed down another of the cinnamon rolls he'd found at Sara's house while he heated up some soup for their supper. Boy, Dillon had been mad when they hadn't found the kid and her mother there after they'd seen the pickup leave.

Willie smiled as he recalled his partner's cursing. Then he sobered. He sure wished he was someplace else.

Chapter Eight

"There." Danielle put the last item in the pantry. The kitchen was neat once more and filled with groceries.

Kyle had helped her clean up, then they had gone to the store to replenish their larder.

"Ready?" he asked.

He stood by the mudroom door, coat in hand, waiting for her. They needed to run by the McCallum house and pick up Sara, then they were going out to dinner. She realized she was tired. The day had been filled with tension—

She shied from thoughts of that morning. Going down to the stables had been her first mistake.

And the next?

Swallowing hard against a strange restless despair that threatened to break her composure, she nodded to Kyle and hurried over to put on her boots and parka.

The next mistake, her conscience insisted, had been giving in to the passion and all that old longing and desire. Why had she allowed that to happen?

Why not take physical satisfaction, a part of her demanded. What did it matter?

She wondered where it had come from, this more cynical self that she'd never known she had until the last couple of months. No, the last couple of years. It was during that time that she had stopped believing…in what?

Kyle?

Herself?

Love?

If my love could hold you… She'd read that somewhere, or heard it, in a book or a song. Her love hadn't been strong enough to hold Kyle. Neither she nor Sara had been enough.

The tears burned her throat, and she fought the terrible need to weep the anguish she'd held inside for weeks and months, years.…

"You look nice," he said in a husky tone.

She had bathed and changed into black wool slacks, a black turtleneck and a black-and-white patterned sweater after they had returned from the old mining camp. She murmured her thanks without looking at him.

"Dani," he said.

"We'd better hurry. Sara will be getting anxious. She worries about things now."

"Things a five-year-old shouldn't have to worry about," he added, his voice much harder.

"Yes." She rushed out the door ahead of him, stopping any further conversation.

In the truck, as they headed for Jenny's house, he was silent, his face dark and closed. Danielle was painfully aware of him. He, too, had bathed and changed. He wore black cords with a white shirt, open at the neck, and a black leather vest under a wool cardigan she had given him their first Christmas. She remembered something else.

"We sent presents to you at the office. For Christmas. Year before last. We didn't do any for you this year since we didn't know…" She hesitated to say that she'd thought he might be dead.

"If I'd ever be home again," he said flatly. "I got the gifts. Luke saved them for me."

He stopped at a light and turned a dark gaze on her. Only one forlorn streetlight and those from the dashboard cast out the winter gloom and highlighted their faces.

"Actually, this all seems surreal to me, as if I might be living in a dream, only I don't know it." She gestured to indicate them and the present moment. But she also meant the past two months and the time he'd been gone.

"You lost your faith in me." His brief laugh was sardonic. "Why wouldn't you? I lost it myself. Sometimes I thought I'd never crawl out of that particular gutter. Sometimes when the night was dark and there wasn't a moon, I thought I'd be lost forever."

She couldn't face the look in his eyes, as if he struggled deep within his soul, as if he wrestled with demons she couldn't begin to comprehend.

"At those moments, I let myself think of you. You

and Sara. Then I'd come back from the brink of madness." He paused, then added, "But then there would be the loneliness to face. It was a toss-up on which was worse."

"I know about the loneliness." Her throat was so tight she could hardly speak. "I know about that. And being abandoned—"

"I never abandoned you," he uttered in a low, angry growl. "Never. I had a job to do. It was too dangerous to involve you and Sara."

She shook her head. "You chose the job over me and Sara. You can justify it because of the danger, but at some point you drew a line. Your family ended up on the other side of that line. We were cut out of your life. Without a word. We weren't part of that choice."

The light changed. He drove on.

She stared out the window as the houses swept by, houses with families inside, warm and happy. She could see them moving about, talking, watching TV, eating dinner.

Outside, in the cold, dark loneliness of night, the truck lights beamed a path down the icy street, its occupants silent on the rest of their trip.

Jessica met Danielle at the door. "The girls behaved quite nicely today. They're putting away the toys now."

"Good."

"Did you find anything at the cabin? Sterling isn't home yet, so I haven't heard anything since you called."

"Kyle said the place had been wiped clean. So had ours, or they wore gloves, which was likely."

"Your place?"

"It was ransacked." Danielle's smile was wry as her friend gasped. "They took most of my groceries. Including some leftover rolls I'd baked this morning."

"Was it the kidnappers?"

Danielle lifted her shoulders and dropped them. "Shane and Rafe think so. Kyle hasn't said." She gathered Sara's parka and book bag. "Thanks for taking Sara home from school with you. I wanted to see the place where she was kept. It was a mining cabin over on the old Baxter place. When she got away, she hid in a cave." Her voice lowered in pain as she envisioned her daughter, cold and frightened, hiding from the men who had terrorized her.

Jessica flashed her a sympathetic glance as they went down the hall to collect the girls.

"Hi," Jenny said brightly when the women entered her room. "Look, we got Sugar dressed up."

Danielle couldn't help but join in Jessica's laughter at the young dog's dilemma. Sugar wore a pink tutu around her middle and a lace puff around her head. She cast the grown-ups a woeful glance, then lay down, her head on her paws, with a heavy sigh.

That brought forth fresh laughter. The girls chimed in.

"We're going to the Hip Hop for dinner. Do you and Jenny want to join us?" Danielle asked.

"Umm, that would be nice. Sterling said not to worry about him since he might be very late."

"Oh, yes, let's go," Jenny seconded the decision.

Sara rose with Jenny and her mom. They followed

the pickup to the café. It was busy, but not crowded, as usual for a Monday night.

They were seated at a large round table near the window. After hats and coats were disposed of, the girls ordered hot cocoa with marshmallows. Danielle decided on hot tea. So did Jessica. Kyle stuck with coffee.

"You have a mustache," Danielle teased Sara after their drinks arrived.

"Your mom used to sport one, too, after she drank cocoa," Kyle confided, leaning toward the youngsters.

Danielle met his gaze and was hit with a searing recollection of drinking cocoa their first winter together, of him licking the rim of chocolate milk off her lips and of all that had followed the simple act.

Heat swept over her in a radiant wave of hunger. She wanted those days again. She wanted to feel alive and needed and desired the way she had in those first glorious years of their marriage. What had happened to change all that?

Not the birth of their daughter. They had wanted a child right away. Sara had added to their marriage, not detracted. The passion and excitement had continued.

Right up until the last night he had come home, weary and cold and bone tired. She had run him a hot bath and let him soak while she prepared a meal. Together they had looked in on the sleeping Sara, then had crept into their bedroom and made love, creating their own glowing world.

Looking back, she thought that night had been different from the previous week when he'd come home briefly for a meal and to pack some clothes. That last night, he'd told her he was going undercover, and she wasn't to speak if she saw him on the street. Then he had made love to her with such intensity it had seared right to her soul. He must have known then he wasn't going to return. It had been goodbye.

Only she hadn't known. She'd waited…and waited…and waited. The faithful Penelope of mythology, weaving her tapestries by day and unraveling them by night, waiting for her adventuring husband to return.

The pain of remembering made her throat ache with unshed tears and all the unspoken words between them.

What use were words? In spite of the episode in the stable that morning, their marriage was effectively over. She must remember that.

"There's Carey," Jessica said. "Hi, Carey, over here. We have room for you."

Dr. Carey Hall Kincaid, Wayne Kincaid's wife, came over. Danielle introduced the pediatrician to Kyle.

Carey spoke and took a seat. "Thanks for including me. I'm here for a quick meal before I go back to the hospital. I'm assisting Kane Hunter in surgery on a patient of mine in a couple of hours."

Jessica made sympathetic sounds, then turned to Kyle. "Carey saved Jenny's life with a bone marrow transplant two years ago. Jen had leukemia and we had almost given up hope."

"Until we found a match in Wayne," Carey noted.

"Only Wayne Kincaid was going under the name J.D. Cade at the time," Jessica informed them. "He didn't want anyone to know he was the legitimate Kincaid heir.''

"He's my brother, only we got different last names 'cause he didn't get adopted like I did,'' Jenny announced proudly. "He gave me some of the inside of his bones.'' She thought intensely for a few seconds. "Mommy said I had to drink my milk because it would give me good bones so I would grow up tall and strong. Will I grow as tall as Wayne?''

"Not likely,'' Carey told the disappointed five-year-old. "Your body has its own plan for how tall you'll be.'' She smiled at Sara. "And how's Miss Sara tonight?''

Sara smiled and ducked her head shyly.

"Still not talking?'' Carey teased lightly.

"Not yet,'' Danielle forced herself to say in the same vein. "But she giggles a lot.''

"Their teacher had to separate these two at school today because they kept giggling,'' Jessica mentioned, looking stern. Then she spoiled it by grinning.

"Giggling, huh? That's good. That's really good.'' The pediatrician nodded approval.

Later when Jessica took the girls to the rest room, Danielle asked Carey if she thought they should do something more for Sara. "Maybe take her to a child psychologist?''

"I'd give it another few weeks. That was pretty traumatic for a child her age. I observed her tonight. She was lively and alert and interested in all that was going on around her. That's normal and all on the plus side. I think she'll be speaking again soon. Let's wait until the end of the month, then reassess the situation, okay?''

"Should we try to talk to her about what happened?" Kyle asked. "I mean, should we insist on it?"

"No, don't push. She's recovering at her own rate. Let's not force it. Discuss it when something comes up on the case, but otherwise let it be." She glanced at her watch. "Oops, got to run. Thanks for letting me share a table with you." She paid at the register and left.

"She's nice," Kyle said. "Seems to have a head on her shoulders. I'm glad Sara has her."

Danielle picked up a pair of gloves. "She forgot these. Can we go by the hospital on the way home and leave them?"

"No problem."

No problem. Danielle sighed. His hand closed over hers for a second. She couldn't hide the sadness she felt when he peered into her face, studying her expression as if delving for some secret she was trying to conceal.

"It will be all right," he said softly. "Things will work out. Then I'll get out of your life for good."

For good. She blinked at that, shocked and hurt anew without knowing why. For a moment, she felt overwhelmed by the double crises in her life—that of the kidnappers and that of her crumbling marriage. Her chest ached as the pressure built inside, but she would rather die than cry in public or in front of the husband who didn't want her in his life anymore.

Swallowing the despair, she nodded and pasted on a smile. "Here come the girls. It's time to go."

After going to the hospital and dropping the gloves

off for the doctor, they returned to the shabby Victorian. A light was on inside.

Danielle frowned. "Did we leave a light on?"

"I don't remember. I'll check out the house. You two stay in the truck. Keep the engine running. Leave if you hear anything that alarms you. Okay?"

She nodded. He turned the truck so it was facing the street before he climbed out and saw her buckled into the driver's seat. Sara watched them, her eyes filled with fear as her father disappeared around the side of the house.

"It's okay," Danielle assured the child with more confidence than she felt. "Daddy will take care of any bad guys. Besides, I'm sure I must have left the light on."

Such a simple thing—leaving a light on, but now it struck terror in her heart. That was perhaps the worst thing criminals did to innocent people—destroyed their sense of security, of being at home in their community. Danielle felt they violated some deep sense of the self, something she had thought was inviolate.

Most of all, she hated it that her child had had to learn distrust of others firsthand. Children should grow up safe in their world.

"It's okay," Kyle called out. "Can you back the truck into the garage?"

"Yes," she called out the window and did so.

Inside, the furnace ducts popped cheerfully as heat spilled into the rooms they used during the winter. The house felt warm and welcoming again. Safe.

She studied Kyle in quick, sideways glances as she

helped Sara prepare for bed. Was it because he said the house was safe that she now felt it was?

"It's already past eight," she said when Sara picked out her favorite book for a bedtime story.

Sara pointed to her father.

"You want Daddy to read it?" Danielle glanced at Kyle who had paused in the doorway. "Would you mind?"

"Not at all," he said with a smile. "Reading about—" he glanced at the title "—the adventures of a magic princess is my kind of fun."

Sara handed Kyle the book, then took Danielle's hand and tugged her across the room. She pointed out where her mom was to sit on the side of the bed, then where her dad was to sit beside them on the floor.

Danielle eased her legs to the side a bit more when his shoulder grazed them. He started reading in his pleasant baritone, putting drama in the story and using different voices for the characters. He was better then she was at this.

She became lost in listening to his voice. Traces of memories floated through her mind like snapshots in an old photo album. Summer days and long walks. Winter nights and a warm body to cuddle up against. The crunch of leaves in the fall. Spring…the time she loved best. When all the world awakened, and flowers bloomed…and all the world fell in love.

Kyle shifted so that her legs became his backrest. She sat as if paralyzed for the remainder of the story. Heat and electricity fizzed up her thighs and into her abdomen. This physical thing was all that was between them now. That was all she felt—a physical attraction.

Finally the story was over. Danielle sighed in relief when Kyle moved. She tucked the covers around Sara, who promptly pulled her arms from under the covers and reached for her parents.

Giving a tug on their sleeves, Sara pulled Kyle and Danielle down so that they could kiss her on each cheek at the same time. It was something they had once done often.

Kyle's cheek brushed hers. She felt the abrasion of his beard, the warmth of his skin. Heat lightning arced from the spot all the way down her spine. She quickly kissed Sara, then pulled back from the electric contact.

Before she could leave, Sara folded her hands under her chin and silently said her prayers. Danielle was swamped with love for their brave little girl and hoped Sara wasn't praying for things that couldn't be.

"Night, love," she whispered.

"Night, punkin," Kyle said at the same time.

He retreated to the doorway while Danielle tucked the covers around Sara again. When she exited, he turned off the light and shut the door, then followed her to the family room.

"I thought I'd catch the news," she said, taking a seat on the sofa, nervous about being alone with him after what had happened that morning. "I want to watch the weather."

"Me, too. We don't need another storm if we're going to catch those guys. If it snows, they'll hole up until the roads are clear again."

"Do you think they'll come back here?"

He moved from window to window, shutting the curtains so no one could see inside. "The burglary could have been someone totally unrelated to the kidnappers.''

"I had assumed it was one and the same." She rubbed her temples where a headache lurked. "I guess there could be more than one set of crooks around." Her laughter sounded strange to her ears.

He stopped behind her. To her surprise, he started rubbing her neck. It was heavenly. He massaged the tension out of the muscles running to the back of her skull, then he rubbed her temples in circular strokes that varied from firm to soft. She closed her eyes.

"I'll give you just thirty minutes to stop that," she managed to say, her voice only slightly shaky.

"Shh," he murmured.

Oh, she shouldn't let him do this. Her resolution not to let him touch her again softened and melted away like a lollipop left out in the rain. She sighed.

He continued rubbing her neck and stroking her temples until she was nearly asleep. She hardly listened when the weather was discussed.

"No storms coming," Kyle said at the end of the announcement. "Good." He sounded pleased.

"The kidnappers will come out of hiding," she murmured. "The sooner you catch them, the sooner you can leave."

His hands tightened momentarily, then resumed their soft stroking. "I talked to Luke while you were in the shower earlier today. He thinks I'll be offered the field office here. They want me to run it."

She stood and faced him. "Here? You'll be staying?"

Her voice was a croak of disbelief. She wasn't

ready for this information. She didn't know how she felt, how she should react...if she could bear it....

His laughter was sardonic. "I can see that doesn't exactly thrill you." He leaned both hands on the back of the sofa. "I'm going to be part of Sara's life. Make up your mind to that."

The question hung in the air—was he also going to be part of hers? "Sara will be thrilled. She loves you very much," she finally said.

He stared into her eyes without speaking. Slowly the challenge in his softened and his expression changed. His gaze became lambent, sexy. The hunger of the morning returned, darkening his eyes to sooty black. Without looking away, he swung his leg over the sofa and slid down onto the cushions. His thigh pressed against her knee.

With one tug, he pulled her into his lap. She didn't protest. She knew she should. But she couldn't. The beat of her heart was too loud. She couldn't hear anything else.

"I've been thinking about your lips," he murmured, his mouth poised above hers. "All day. Give me your magic kiss. Make me whole again."

The words made no sense, but the intensity did. It matched that within herself. To her shame, she didn't fight him. Instead, she lifted her face to his and gave him the kiss he asked for.

It was bliss. It was foolish beyond measure. It was heaven. It was dying and being reborn.

She pushed her fingers into the dark strands of his hair and held him closer. She didn't question the rightness or fairness of the hunger, only that it was there between them and it hurt more to resist than to give in.

At this moment.

"I'll think about tomorrow when it comes," she mused aloud when the kiss ended.

"Don't think about it at all," he advised. "It only makes you ache for all the promises that won't be filled."

She snuggled her face into the groove of his neck and shoulder. "Have all your promises been lies?"

"Not all." He kissed the side of her face, nuzzled along her neck and ear. "Whatever I said to you…it was never a lie. I've never lied to you."

"But when you left…?" Her voice trailed off into a question.

"I had to. I had to," he repeated.

She pressed her face against him and sighed. "Let's not talk about it. It doesn't help."

Kyle felt the hot scalding tears against his neck. Dani was crying? "I never meant to bring you anything but happiness," he tried to explain.

"Then how could you leave like that? Without a word. With no explanation. I thought you'd be back. I needed you. But you never came. Never."

"Shh. I know." He ran his hands over her back, into her hair. He tried to tell her with his touch how much he regretted hurting her. Maybe he had made a mistake in not allowing her to make the choice.

No, he knew her. She would have chosen to be with him, no matter the danger. She and Sara could have been killed. And that he couldn't allow.

"I can't go back. I can't change—"

She was out of his arms in a flash. "No, you can't.

Neither can I. Not that much. You just can't walk back into the house and into the life we had. It's gone.''

The pit of darkness stirred inside him. "I know," he said. "I knew it when I walked out."

He couldn't face the pain, the stark and dreadful hurt that lay exposed in her eyes. He hadn't realized it would hurt her so much. She had had all that love inside, that deep quiet well of peace, to draw from.

It was what he had called on at his blackest moments. He had used her strength to keep going in the fight for justice. "If I hadn't stuck it out, we would have never been safe," he found himself explaining. "You and Sara and I...we would have always had to be on the run, always looking over our shoulders for the chance encounter with the one person who could identify me. I couldn't take that chance."

She let out a shaky breath. "I know." Her smile broke his heart. "I understand, truly I do. You had to go on with your work. It's important. I know that. A family only holds you back." She left him with that thought.

Long after Danielle was in bed, and the house was quiet, he sat in the dark and digested her words. The one time his family had truly needed him, he hadn't been available.

He had been so intent on his mission that he had ignored all distractions, even Luke's summons to come to the office. He had succeeded in closing his case, but he had failed as a husband and a father.

Chapter Nine

Danielle woke with a sneeze the next morning. Her head hurt and her throat was raw. Kyle took one look at her when she entered the kitchen and told her to sit down. He poured a cup of coffee and a glass of orange juice and brought them to her at the table.

"I'll walk Sara to school this morning," he said. "You stay in and nurse that cold. You got any echinacea?"

"No."

"I'll pick up some in town."

She gave him a baleful glance, then ignored him. He grinned in that maddening male way that said he had everything under control. To her surprise, he proceeded to get Sara up and ready for school, including fixing her breakfast and supervising brushing her teeth.

Sara pointed to her hair just before they headed out the door and shook her head.

"It looks fine," Kyle told her. He'd parted it to one side and put in a barrette to hold it out of her eyes. The barrette was already slipping.

Sara shook her head firmly and pulled the unruly curls into a bunch at the back of her neck.

"She wants a ponytail," Danielle explained.

"Is that what you want?" Kyle asked the youngster.

Sara nodded.

"Then you have to tell me." He dropped to his haunches. "Tell me what you want, Sara. You can talk. Tell me."

The room fell to instant silence.

"Kyle," Danielle began.

He waved her to silence. "It's okay to talk, Sara. You don't have to be afraid, not of Mommy and Daddy."

Danielle's mouth dried up as the tension mounted. Sara's eyes seemed to fill her face. She placed both hands over her mouth and shook her head, slowly, then faster.

"Sara—"

"Kyle, please don't force her—"

"I'm not going to force her to do anything," he said softly. He leaned close to Sara. "You know we love you, don't you?"

The five-year-old hesitated, then nodded.

"You have nothing to fear. You're here at home. It's safe here. You're safe here, Sara." He lifted her into his arms and rose. "I'll never let anyone hurt you. That's a promise, okay?"

She nodded again.

He looked over at Danielle. "That's a promise," he repeated, his eyes locked with hers.

She wanted to tell him not to make promises he couldn't keep, but something held her silent. It seemed important to him that she believe him, too.

And she did. In as much as it was in his power to do so, he would keep them from harm. She didn't doubt that he would give his life for them. If only he would also share it with them.

When she nodded, he set Sara on the stool and left them for a moment. Danielle studied her daughter. The fear had gone, and the child seemed deep in thought. Danielle wished she could get some vibes the way Winona Cobbs did. Maybe she would know how to help Sara then.

Right now, all she felt was the pain of breathing. She sipped the coffee and let the heat soothe the raw flesh of her throat.

Kyle returned with a brush and hair band. "Okay, Operation Ponytail coming up."

Sara grinned.

He brushed the fine blond hair into a bundle in his left hand, then worked the band on carefully. The pony fell into an untidy mess on the nape of Sara's neck.

"You have to hold it tight and get the band right down to her scalp."

"I'm afraid I'll pull."

"Sara's used to that. You have to keep it tight. Wrap the band around your fingers several times before you slip it on."

He brushed the curls into a relatively smooth bundle again. After wrapping the band around his fingers, he tried to get it over the bunch before it fell apart.

"Well, I got half of it in," he said, surveying the results with a critical eye.

Sara giggled. Danielle had to smile as he frowned and started over.

"You have to grab her hair right at the scalp with the fingers the band is on," she suggested helpfully. She made little grabby motions with her fingers in a circle.

This time he looked seriously determined as he doubled, then tripled the hair band around the fingers of his right hand. He held the ponytail in place with his left hand, then grabbed the hair next to the scalp.

"Ha, just like wrestling a snake," he declared. "You got to get it right behind the head."

"Now pull the band over the hair with your left hand while you hold on for dear life with the right and pull it through," Danielle directed.

"Got it!" He finished the chore while Sara winced a bit but remained silent.

He looked so proud that Danielle couldn't help but laugh. Sara checked her hair with both hands, then beamed at her dad. Their smiles were very much alike, father and daughter. Danielle had to look away as her heart acted up.

After the other two left, she took a shower, which unclogged her stuffy nose and made her feel better. She dressed, took two aspirin and two multiple vitamins, then lay on the sofa and watched clouds gather over the mountain peaks west of town.

Snow, she thought with a shiver. Her eyes drifted shut, and she dozed until she heard an engine in the driveway. She recognized the truck and its driver. Kyle had returned.

Peace fell over her. She felt better having him home. She listened to his movements when he entered the house. She knew when he bent over her and tucked an afghan around her. She heard him build a fire in the grate and knew when he closed the curtains, all without opening her eyes.

She slept heavily after that.

The jarring ring of the telephone woke her up. She sat straight up and threw off the afghan, alarm running through her. Kyle answered the phone in the kitchen before she could reach for the one on the end table.

"Danielle?" he called. "You'd better pick up."

Her hand trembled as she lifted the receiver. "Yes? Who is it?"

"It's Lynn. From school. The principal and I are in the office with Sara. She's crying—"

"What's wrong?" Danielle demanded. "What happened?"

"We don't know. The kids went out for their recess as usual. She was fine then. Jenny and Sara and two other girls jumped rope, then rested on a bench at the corner of the playground. The four of them got up to play on the gym. Jenny and Sara went to the water fountain. It was odd. She was fine one minute, then the next she was running and shaking and crying. I took her into the classroom. She went to her seat, put both hands over her mouth and sat there crying. She hasn't stopped."

"Where was Rawlings during all this?" Kyle wanted to know.

"He had checked the grounds and everything out this morning, then he had to go to court on another case. He's back now. He's questioning some of the kids."

"I'll be right there," Danielle said. "Would you stay with Sara until I arrive? She trusts you."

"Of course," Lynn assured her. "She's really upset, almost hysterical."

In the background, Danielle could hear the principal speaking in soothing tones. She couldn't hear Sara. "Okay. Tell her that Mommy is on the way."

"And Daddy," Kyle added grimly.

Danielle hung up and dashed to the kitchen. Kyle was already putting on his coat. She pulled on her boots and grabbed her coat. "Let's go."

"Wait. I want to set the detectors."

She hit the button to open the garage door, grabbed her purse and found the keys to her car while she ran down the slippery path. Before she could get inside, Kyle caught up with her.

"Get in the truck," he ordered.

She jumped in without arguing. He took off, the back tires throwing a plume of slushy snow behind them. At the school, he parked near the door. Danielle jumped out and raced to the office, Kyle on her heels.

Danielle burst into the room without knocking. Lynn and the principal were kneeling on the floor beside Sara. Sara was sitting in a chair, her knees drawn up to her chest, her face hidden behind her hands. Her head flew up, terror on her tear-streaked face, when Danielle and Kyle entered.

Sara held out her arms. Sobs racked her small body. Her mouth opened. "M-mommy!" she cried.

Danielle caught her daughter to her and held her tight. "There, darling, there. It's okay. Mommy's here. And Daddy."

Sara had a stranglehold on her neck. One arm loosened and she held it out to Kyle. "Daddy! Don't leave me!"

Kyle closed his arms around Sara and Danielle. He crushed both of them to him. "I won't leave you, Sara. Not ever. Promise."

Danielle dropped her head back and stared up at him, tears in her eyes. "She spoke," she said softly, not sure it wasn't her imagination. "Sara spoke."

He nodded and blinked his eyes rapidly. "Let's see if we can sort this out," he suggested after giving them another collective hug. "Maybe we should sit down."

Danielle's legs were definitely shaky. She took the chair Sara had vacated and settled Sara on her lap. The other three adults arranged themselves in a semi-circle around them.

"Sara, something scared you," Kyle began. "Can you tell me what it was?"

Sara shook her head and stared into her lap. She sniffed. Danielle dug a tissue from her pocket and held it while Sara blew her nose.

Kyle laid a reassuring hand on Sara's knee. "You have to talk, sweetheart. This is important."

Danielle forced herself to borrow some of Kyle's infinite patience and sit still. She felt the tremors that coursed through Sara and hated the men who had done this to a child.

"I'm not supposed to," Sara said at last.

"Who said you weren't supposed to talk?" Kyle asked in an interested tone.

Another silence. Finally Sara murmured, "The bad man."

Kyle nodded solemnly. "He had no right to tell you that. Mommy and I are the only ones who can tell you never to talk. Your teacher can tell you to be quiet when you're here at school, but no one else can tell you to do things unless Mommy or I say it's okay first. No one, understand?"

Sara looked at Danielle who nodded.

"Okay." She still didn't sound totally convinced.

"What did you see?" Kyle asked. "What scared you?"

Sara bit her lip. She sighed heavily as if giving up a worrisome burden. "It was the bad man. Dillon. He's mean and he has a snake tattoo. He said he'd come and…and hurt Mommy if I ever told about him and Willie."

Dillon. Willie. Danielle's blood ran cold. Those were the men Shane and Rafe had mentioned. Dillon Pierce. Partner to Angela McBride's former husband. Willie Sparks, a local ne'er-do-well.

"I won't let anyone hurt Mommy," Kyle promised.

"He said he'd kill her…and cut out my tongue, so I'd better not say anything," Sara continued, her eyes wide.

Danielle saw the muscles contract in Kyle's arm and knew he was feeling the same as she was. She would have gladly strangled the man if he'd been at hand.

"He won't hurt anyone," Kyle stated in a voice that inspired confidence.

Danielle felt the tension seep out of the child.

Sara glanced at Lynn. "You couldn't see him. He was hiding behind the corner of the building when I went to get a drink of water. He said I had to go with him. But I didn't," she said proudly. "I went to the teacher like Mommy said I should if anything happened."

"You did exactly right," Danielle assured her.

"Absolutely," Lynn echoed, her face grim.

The principal shook her head. "But we've been so careful. How could he have gotten on the property without being seen?"

"He looked like Mr. Rafe," Sara explained. "He weared, I mean, wore the same clothes and a cap."

"He was dressed as a custodian," Kyle concluded, his face expressionless. "How many men are usually here?"

"Two. And both of them were painting in one of the temporary classrooms. I was talking to them about how long before we could use the room when the secretary buzzed me on my pager. Lynn was in the office with Sara when I arrived."

Kyle stood. "It's easy enough to get coveralls and a cap and look official. The guy is getting bolder."

Or more desperate, Danielle thought. He wanted the money he thought Angela had. And he needed to silence Sara so he couldn't be identified. But by who else, besides Sara.

"He has to be known to someone else around here," she said aloud. "Otherwise why be so worried about a five-year-old? They wouldn't likely meet on the street, especially during school hours.''

"Exactly," Kyle said. "He needs to know if the police are already on to him."

His eyes met hers, and she knew he was ahead of her. He had already figured that out.

"Are they?" Lynn asked.

Kyle nodded. "Dillon Pierce. We suspected him almost from the first. He had motive—a million dollars Angela's first husband embezzled and Dillon thinks Angela has. He followed her to Whitehorn and hooked up with Willie."

"Willie was nice," Sara said suddenly. "He got my favorite cereal for breakfast, and he played cards with me. Dillon was mean. He was always mad."

Danielle hugged her. "Well, he'd better watch himself. He's in big trouble."

"Are you going to put him in jail?" Sara asked her father.

His grin was sardonic. "You bet."

"When you catch him, then he'll be sorry."

"Right," Kyle agreed. "He'll be very sorry."

"I think there'll be a line of men wanting to speak to the man once he's caught," Lynn said. "You and Sterling McCallum, Jenny's father. Shane. Rafe. Ross has mentioned what he'd like to do to men who would take a child."

Ross Garrison, her very new husband, was an attorney. He'd been worried that Lynn might be the target the men were after for some reason, that they might have attacked the wrong woman just as they'd taken the wrong child. Having Sara in her class had put her in danger, too.

Lynn and Ross and Danielle had talked about the complications, along with Sterling and Jessica. Lynn had insisted she wasn't afraid to take Sara back into her classroom. Ross had agreed it was best for Sara and the right thing to do. He, too, kept an eye out for strangers hanging around the school or their house.

They were good people. Danielle's heart filled with gratitude. In spite of the kidnapping, she felt more and more that Whitehorn was a good place for her and Sara. It was less lonely than the city had been without Kyle.

"Shall I take Sara back to class now?" Lynn asked. "It's almost time for a story, her favorite thing."

Danielle looked at Kyle. He thought it over. "The guy isn't going to risk coming back today. It's probably better that she stick with routine."

Lynn held out her hand to Sara. "Ready?"

Sara slid off Danielle's lap. "What story are we going to have today?" she wanted to know. The two of them walked out, Sara chatting almost normally.

The difference, Danielle noted, was that once Sara would have been dancing ahead while she chattered. Now she walked close beside her teacher, Lynn's hand firmly in hers.

"I want to look around," Kyle told the principal. "But first, I want to talk to Rafe." He headed out the door.

The principal gestured to Danielle. "Let's go make a pot of tea. One of the teachers brought in homemade biscotti. That would hit the spot, wouldn't it, after the scare this morning?"

Danielle stayed in the teacher's lounge while Kyle

and Rafe went over every inch of the school grounds, then the grounds outside the fence. Other than a set of footprints that indicated the man might have climbed over the fence, they didn't find anything remotely suspicious, he reported when he collected Sara and Danielle at noon.

They went home. She sighed in relief when they reached the house. "You rest," he said once they were inside. "I'll heat some soup for lunch, then Sara and I will be as quiet as mice. You won't know we're on the place."

"What am I supposed to be doing while you're creeping around on tippy-toe?"

"Taking a nap. You sound like a frog with a grasshopper stuck in its throat."

"Thanks," she croaked, but she went in and lay down on the sofa, feeling as tired as if she'd split logs all day.

"And they lived happily ever after in their enchanted land far away," Kyle read and closed the book.

Sara, sitting in the bathtub with her plastic dolls, sighed. "Do you think I'll ever find a prince who will think I'm the beautifulest one of all?" she asked wistfully.

"Of course you will," he said automatically.

"Well, I'm not pretty like Jenny." She laid her princess and prince dolls on a doll-size float—it had taken him a while to get used to his daughter playing with totally naked boy and girl dolls—then propped her chin on her hand. "She's got dimples."

Kyle started to reassure his daughter, but when he

looked into her eyes, he couldn't brush aside her concerns.

Neither could he lie. Jenny McCallum was one of those children who are born beautiful. Along with blond hair and blue eyes with naturally dark lashes, she had a perfectly chiseled face, a rosebud mouth and, as Sara had noted, dimples so cute that people exclaimed about them when she smiled.

By contrast, Sara, who also had blond hair and blue eyes, had gamine features. Her face was broad across the cheeks and tapered quickly to a sharp little chin. Her mouth was wide and her nose was short. As she had noted, she had no dimples. A little cat face.

Like her mother's.

A fist closed around his heart and squeezed hard. He tried to think carefully of what he should say to young Sara. "There're different kinds of beauty," he began.

She nodded glumly. "Mommy says beauty is as beauty does. Outside beauty doesn't last very long, but inside beauty lasts forever."

"That's true." He nodded wisely and tried to think of something to add. Sweat broke out on his face. "Some movie stars are beautiful people, but we wouldn't like them if we knew them because they're not kind or thoughtful."

"Yeah. But Jerry Smith likes Jenny."

Ah. Now he understood the problem. "Some people fall for a pretty face," he consoled her.

"Jenny is very nice," Sara defended her friend.

Okay, maybe the movie star analogy hadn't been a good one. "Well, sure. So are you."

He wished Danielle would come in and rescue him

from this conversation. He was afraid he was saying all the wrong things. The sweat collected into droplets. He wiped his face with a towel.

She sighed. "But she's beautiful outside and inside. How does anybody see my insides?"

She gazed up at him earnestly, waiting for his words of wisdom. None came to mind. "Well," he said and thought hard. He wiped his face again. Must be the steam that was making him sweat.

"How did you see Mommy's?" Sara asked.

Kyle thought back to that cold winter evening when Danielle had told him the library was closing. They were the last two people in the place. He'd noticed her earlier when she'd helped him find the information he'd needed.

The two flagrantly nude dolls floating on their swim mattress bobbed against Sara's knee. She called the float a magic carpet.

"It's sort of like magic," he said slowly, savoring the memory. "I took one look and I noticed right off there was something special about her."

Her smile. Her competence. The light in her eyes, the quiet center of her that had made him want to sink into her and bask in the warmth...the peace....

"What?" Sara wanted to know.

"I thought she was beautiful."

"You did?"

"Yes," he said huskily, remembering how he'd wanted to touch her hair, its auburn strands surrounding her face in curling tendrils like dark flames. He bent and studied Sara. "You have my eyes, but you have your mom's face. A little cat face."

Doubt entered Sara's eyes again. "Huh," she said.

"Kittens are cute," he hurriedly added, wiping his forehead on his sleeve. The bathroom sure seemed hot. "And when they grow up, they become lovely and graceful cats. Have you noticed the way a cat moves, how smooth and beautiful it is?"

She nodded slowly, her forehead knit in thought.

"So when I met Mommy, I saw all those things— how graceful she was, how kind she was in helping me, and I thought, now there's a beautiful woman. And that's the way I saw her. And still do."

Sara nodded. "'Cause Mommy is beautiful."

"Someday some guy is going to look at you and he'll think you're the most beautiful woman he ever saw."

She picked up her prince doll and stared at him intently. "When?"

"Well, that's the mystery of it. And the romance. One day, when you're all grown-up, you'll meet someone. You'll look into his eyes and you'll know he's your prince."

Sara tossed the prince doll into the water. He landed facedown and slowly sank. "Daddy," Sara said wisely, sadly, "princes and princesses are just a fairy tale."

"Maybe." Now he was on the defensive. "But wait until you meet the right one. You'll change your mind. Now you'd better get out of the water before you turn into a wrinkled old witch with a wart on her nose."

Sara thought that was really funny. She giggled about it until she was in bed and he turned out the light and reminded her sternly that it was quiet time.

Danielle was sitting up on the sofa when he entered

the family room. A fire licked merrily over the logs in the fireplace. A television was on, but the sound was muted. The scene was straight out of Currier and Ives.

"That was very nice," she said. "What you said to Sara," she explained when he questioned her with a glance.

"Yeah, well, just don't expect me to explain the birds and bees to her."

She laughed, a sort of sexy croak. A low thrum vibrated through his body.

He noticed she had changed into one of the long flannel nightgowns she preferred in winter. He recalled how soft the material was when he slid his palm slowly along her waist and hip, exploring those wonderful feminine curves. He stared into the fire and tried to force the memories at bay.

Rising, he prowled restlessly from window to window, checking that the house was secure, that the motion detectors were in place and working. He left off the one in the hall. He didn't know if Danielle would go to bed or sleep on the sofa. She'd taken a hot shower and some cold pills after dinner—another soup-and-sandwich meal—and sounded somewhat better than she had earlier.

All seemed quiet outside. The moon reflected brightly off the snow in the fields around the house. He approved the location. There were neighbors, but they weren't too close.

In the field behind the house were patches of woods and outcroppings of rocks—great places for kids to explore and play pirates or cowboys. Or house, if that's what girls played. And castles and knights and princesses. Sara loved stories of enchanted princesses.

A wry smile pulled at the corners of his mouth. Sara was going to be a pragmatist. She had put him straight on fairy tales and reality. He returned to the family room and added a log to the fire.

Danielle had changed channels to a classical concert with the Boston Pops. The music wafted softly around them. Like golden threads of sound that wove magic...

He sat on the raised brick hearth and punched at the fire, then put the poker up. Turning, he let his eyes feast on Danielle.

His wife. The one person he hadn't been afraid to let into the darkness of his soul. Sometimes he thought she had saved him from hell. And there had been times when he knew she had. Those two years...the abandonment she would never forgive. He could see it in her eyes.

Dani no longer trusted him with her heart.

But watching her as she gazed into the fire, the flames licked along his veins. He hadn't lied to Sara. Dani was beautiful in his eyes. She always would be.

"You've done a good job with Sara," he told her. "She's a kid to be proud of. How many five-year-olds could keep silent as long as she has to protect those she loves?"

He shook his head and felt the unexpected smart of tears against his eyelids. His women were brave. Dani and Sara had faced terror alone while he was off on his personal crusade to rid the world of evil. It came to him that he didn't have to fight all those battles alone.

Her sigh stilled the remorse. She twiddled a curl between her finger and thumb, over and over. A chasm opened inside him.

She was the only woman he had ever wanted in this way, with an ache that made his teeth hurt, with a seriousness that bound his heart to hers, with a longing that excluded all other women. The thrum in his blood grew louder.

She had taken him into her home and made it his. She had poured her love, her light, her peace into him.

"Dani," he said.

Every nerve in Danielle's body reacted to her name on his lips. Dani. Only he had ever called her that, and only in the privacy of their lovemaking. She forced herself to look at him and then wished she hadn't.

His eyes were dark and dangerously seductive. Tension filled the air between them and vibrated with suppressed urgency. He wanted her. And God help her, she wanted him.

"No," she said on an exhaled breath.

His smile was brief but lucid. She caught the irony of his thoughts. It hadn't been necessary for her to respond. He knew it was impossible.

But the longing was still there. She clutched her hands in her lap. Need clamored through her. She recalled how wonderful it had been to touch him the other day, to stop fighting and simply take....

No, that would be foolish.

But why not?

She would wonder, later, if something in her face gave her away. But when he rose and came to her, she didn't protest. She simply watched as he dropped to the sofa beside her. She didn't move when he caressed her cheek with his fingertips.

When he drew a line across her lips, she had to open her mouth in order to breathe.

"I'm afraid," she murmured. This could hurt too much. She shouldn't get entangled again so that she learned to depend on him.

"You think I'm not?" His smile was gently mocking.

"You've never been afraid of anything."

He bent toward her, his mouth drawing nearer and nearer until she felt his breath on her face. "You scare me to death."

"Don't lie," she said, the anger rising.

"Men can kill my body," he said. "But you...you can destroy my soul."

Chapter Ten

Danielle stared into Kyle's eyes. She saw no humor there, only the relentless darkness that made her afraid. For him, she realized. Something had changed in him during the time he'd been gone. It was as if he'd been to hell and narrowly escaped, as if it had taken all that he was as a man to make it back from that ghastly brink.

"Dani," he murmured.

She heard the need he couldn't express, the hunger he couldn't deny. The familiar ache entered her chest, making it difficult to breathe, to think. She started to speak, then bit back the words, unsure what to say.

"Mommy!"

Every nerve in her body jerked at the sound of Sara's tremulous voice. Kyle drew back. They rose as one and headed for the bedroom. Inside, she found Sara tossing relentlessly in a troubled dream.

"Shh, I'm here," Danielle murmured, smoothing the curls around Sara's face. "It's okay."

Sara stared up at her. Her frightened gaze went to Kyle. Danielle felt the tension leave the small body.

"Daddy's here," Sara said. "Now it's okay."

Kyle leaned over Danielle's shoulder to rub Sara's back. "Yeah, I'm here. Go back to sleep. I'm keeping an eye on things."

Sara yawned and turned on her side, convinced that all was right with her world. Danielle tucked the covers under Sara's chin and continued to smooth her curls while Kyle rubbed her back. In a minute, the child was sound asleep.

Danielle dropped her hands into her lap and studied her daughter. She was suddenly aware that Kyle was in her bedroom, that his chest still pressed against her shoulder as he continued to rub their child. That funny, achy need to cry came over her.

She moved, indicating it was time to go. He stepped back. They returned to the family room.

"Are you going to sleep here tonight?" he asked, nodding toward the sofa.

"Yes. It's easier to breathe partially sitting up. I don't want to wake Sara in case I start coughing."

The excuse sounded lame. She didn't know why she felt compelled to explain herself, anyway. She frowned.

"You need a vaporizer."

"I don't know where it is."

"I do. It's upstairs in a box."

While he went to get it, she arranged two pillows

on the sofa and lay down, weary to the bone. She kept her eyes closed when she heard Kyle return. In a moment, the gentle hiss of the vaporizer added to the crackle of the fire.

The house fell silent and she went to sleep. An hour later she woke with a start. She listened avidly, then slumped into the pillow. It had been a dream. She wasn't trapped in the cave in the mountains with the voices of the kidnappers coming toward her.

Rolling her head to the side, she gazed at the fire. A silhouette partially blocked her view.

Kyle.

He sat in the recliner, his feet propped on the hearth. Like a lone sentinel against the night and its dangers, he stared into the dancing flames, his features sharply etched in firelight and shadows.

A sense of security washed over her, obliterating the fear caused by the dream. He was protection enough against the dark forces.

She smiled at the fanciful idea. But the truth was, she did feel safer with him there. Longing pierced all the way through her. She wished they could go back to another time, a time when they'd been happy.

He was her husband. Her only lover. All her plans for the future had included him. Then he'd left.

That fact sank into the bottomless pit that had opened inside her when she'd finally accepted that he wasn't going to come back. He'd explained about the danger, but she didn't understand. She could no more abandon him and Sara than she could cut off her arm. It was simply unthinkable.

The ache of tears added to all her other aches. She sighed shakily. He turned his head.

"You awake?" he asked softly.

"Yes." The word was a croak.

"A hot salt water gargle would soothe your throat. I'll fix you a glass." He started to rise.

"No, that's okay. I'll do it." She hurried to the bathroom. After brushing her teeth, taking some cold medication, then gargling with the salt water, she did feel better. The need to cry gradually dissipated.

Returning to the family room, she found her pillows fluffed and the afghan neatly folded back. Kyle arranged two new logs in the fire and settled in the chair again. She sat in the corner of the sofa and tucked her feet under the cover. Then she studied him and wondered why a man like him, a loner, a crusader against evil, would have been attracted to her, a plain, quiet sort of person, in the first place.

As if sensing her perusal, he turned his head. When their eyes locked, an electric bolt sizzled through her. All her senses sharpened and refocused on the tension that arced between them. She couldn't look away.

Finally, his gaze dropped from hers. She watched as his eyes roamed over her, pausing at her mouth, her breasts rising fitfully under the warm material of her gown, the outline of her legs that were folded to one side and tucked close to her body. When he looked into her eyes again, she saw stark hunger and a restless need so great, it couldn't be denied. Neither could hers.

Without looking away, he rose and came to her. Without a word, he sat beside her. Then he stared into her eyes again, and she saw there was only one question.

Yes, some part of her answered before she could think.

When his face dipped toward her, she felt she had to speak. "I have a cold." She sounded breathless and unsure.

"It doesn't matter."

His voice was deep, husky, sexy. It joined the rush of blood through her ears, drowning out all other sounds.

"Dani," he said.

Perhaps if he hadn't said her name in just that way, perhaps if he hadn't laid his hands on her shoulders with that exquisite gentleness he had, perhaps then she could have said no.

She closed her eyes instead, afraid of the hunger she saw in his and of the answer she found in herself.

The kiss was soft, barely a touch. And so sweet, so unbearably, heartbreakingly sweet. Tears filled her eyes behind her closed lids. She lifted her arms to him like a child wanting to be held.

His arms glided around and under her. He swung her up and settled her across his lap. With one hand, he coaxed her head to his shoulder. This was madness. She should run, save herself from the pain of loving him again, then his lips touched hers once more.

She felt his fingers burrow into her hair and cup the back of her head. Heat flowed and mingled between them. Her breasts pressed into his chest. Her hips snuggled into the angle of his hips and thighs. Their lips touched hungrily in a thousand ways—teasing, demanding, cruel, gentle, angry, sad....

A log fell apart. The fire blazed, then settled. The wind piped notes in the eaves of the old house.

The seconds stretched to minutes, to eternity. She couldn't get enough. She held his head between her hands and drank as deeply as she could from this magic nectar.

She couldn't breathe, but she didn't really need to. He was all she needed at this moment. He broke the rapacious contact of their mouths and pressed his face into her neck.

"It's been hell," he whispered hoarsely. "To hell and beyond, but you were always there. Always."

She soothed him as she would young Sara, with sounds and half murmured assurances, with all the comforting touches she'd ever known. Gradually the tension changed as physical hunger replaced the emotional.

"I want to see you," he said urgently. "I've lived on dreams. Now I need..."

His hands, his mouth, showed her his needs. At some point the buttons of her gown mysteriously opened. He planted kisses along her collarbone and down to the swell of her breasts. She whimpered when he suckled there.

"The hunger," she whispered. "It hurts. I want...but I shouldn't—"

"I know," he said. He pushed the heavy tresses away from her face. "You make me ache. You fill me with hunger for things only you can satisfy."

Somehow she knew he hungered for more than her body. He needed more. She wasn't sure she could fill the abyss she sensed inside him. Fear tugged at her. She didn't think she could be all he needed her to be.

She tried to think, to be the responsible one. "Sara—"

"The alarm will go off if she enters the hall," he murmured, biting and nuzzling along her neck, sending curls of passion through her until even her toes tingled.

"Is this wise?" she asked desperately.

"Dani."

Her name was a plea. He touched her cheek with fingers that trembled slightly. His breath sighed over her as he gazed into her eyes with a longing so harsh, so wild, it shocked her.

She hadn't known he could need her like that.

All doubts burned to ash in that hot, imploring gaze. She slid her arms around his chest and hugged him as hard as she could. A wild, fierce joy spread over her. She could give him this.

"Come to me," she commanded, implored. "Come to me."

"I have protection," he told her. "If we need it."

"I'm still on birth control."

"I had wondered…after two years."

He could have checked her medicine cabinet, but he had respected her privacy. She marveled at this man she had married so precipitously. He was a frustrating enigma in some ways, but he was the man she loved. She squeezed her eyes shut. Yes, she loved him. Still.

He opened the remaining buttons on her old-fashioned nightgown. He admired her figure with a searing perusal. Then he stripped the sweat suit from his own lean, rock-hard body and reached for her.

The magic grew and filled her heart. The room

glowed in the firelight, and their shadows danced upon the walls as they shifted and turned, exploring all the variations on the theme of passion that played between them.

She sat astride and rode until he pulled her against him, panting for control. He rolled her beneath him and thrust until she cried out in need.

"Dani," he said on a gasp. "Be still."

But she couldn't. "Now," she demanded, dropping love bites along his shoulder. "Now, now, yes, *now.*"

He came to her in wave after wave of blinding delight. The world condensed to them, just them, and the magic points where they touched, and there was nothing else…no, nothing.

Kyle lay against the sofa. Danielle, asleep, was tucked against him, her back to his chest, his knees cupped into the back of hers. He listened to the sounds of the old house, its whispering and groaning, and to the almost noiseless crackle of the fire as it burned down to embers.

At this moment his family was safe, and Dani was in his arms again. He wished tomorrow would never come.

But it would, and with it, the inevitable questions, the ones he saw in Dani's eyes whenever she wasn't on guard against him. The fact was, she didn't trust him anymore. By leaving, he had forfeited any right to expect either trust or love. He had accepted that fact, and the act of love didn't mean everything was okay again. It was her call.

When the room cooled, he eased off the sofa and, after hitting the remote to turn off the alarm system, went to the bathroom. He refilled the vaporizer, checked on Sara, made a tour of the house and rebuilt the fire. Finally he sat in the recliner and pondered the future.

He thought of living in this house with Dani and Sara. There were a thousand improvements he could make to the place. He found himself eager to do them. And there was the job heading up the field office. Not as exciting as undercover work, but it was time he hung up his spurs, so to speak, and became the man his family needed.

If Dani would have him.

She had made love with him, but she, too, had gone two years without physical release. Add that to the terror of the past couple of months and it was no wonder she'd reacted passionately. So lovemaking didn't count. Not yet.

He wanted more. He wanted to be in her bed, but also in her heart. And that was closed against him.

Well, there it was—the cold, stark truth. He'd known he was taking a chance when he'd decided he had to cut them out of his life for their safety, but he hadn't realized how high the price would be. He hadn't figured on living with the regret hour by hour, day by day. And the loss. How did a man live when half his soul had died?

He had no right to ask anything from her. But he wanted it all, everything she'd once given him freely from her generous heart. He needed the deep inner peace she gave to him. It was for her and Sara that he wanted to rid the world of crime lords, kidnappers, drug dealers—the slimy underbelly of society.

But he had to give something back. That's where

he'd failed. As a wife, a mother, as a human being, Dani had needs, too. And he had failed her in all of them.

"What time is it?" she asked, startling him. She sat up and pushed the tangles from her face.

He had always liked seeing her first thing in the morning when he opened his eyes. He used to lie in bed and watch her sleep. She'd always been self-conscious that her hair wasn't combed and she wasn't fancied up, but she was a symbol of all that was right in his world.

"Nearly four."

"You should go to bed. You don't sleep very much."

He wasn't surprised that she had noticed. She was like that. "Will you come with me?" he asked, then was surprised by the question. He hadn't known that was what he was thinking, but he wanted her there, in bed beside him.

The firelight cast mysterious shadows in her eyes. Sometimes, when the light hit them right, the golden flecks gleamed, reminding him of the treasure he had once had, and that he had lost. He held his breath, waiting...

"I suppose I had better go to bed. Sara might awaken—"

"With me," he interjected. "Will you sleep with me?"

The question hovered in the air between them, naked with his need and yearning. He suddenly knew it didn't matter. He was past masculine posturing. Some things were more important than pride. He wouldn't take the question back.

Her gaze dropped to her lap. She studied the sofa where they had made love, then she looked at him again. Slowly, obviously unsure if this was the right thing, she nodded.

"If...if you think..."

"I do."

Without giving her a chance to think it over, he closed the fire screen, then ushered her down the hall and into the room he'd claimed, the one that was meant to be the master suite, the one he intended to share with her from now on.

"It's cold in here," she whispered in a laughing protest. She pulled the covers back and climbed into the bed. "Didn't you open the vents?"

"No, but I will." He adjusted the vents so warm air would circulate into the room. "Next year I'll install a new duct system. And air conditioning. After I get the windows replaced and the insulation in."

She pulled the covers up to her chin, her face thoughtful while he stripped from his sweats and climbed into bed. He reset the alarm and laid the remote control on the table he'd found in the attic.

"That's a lot of work," she said after a lengthy pause.

"I'll be here," he said. "I've decided to take the job in Whitehorn if it's offered."

"Managing the field office?" She was skeptical. "It's all paperwork. You'll hate it."

He pulled her into his arms, ravaged by her doubts. "You'll see," he said quietly. "I promise. You'll see."

She sighed and said no more, but he sensed the doubts that plagued her. He would change all that.

"I'm home, Dani," he murmured. Peace stole over him like a leaf falling gently into his soul.

Danielle tried not to glance too frequently at Kyle as she prepared oatmeal and English muffins for breakfast. She blushed each time she met his eyes. Then he would smile in that maddening way men have when they've had great sex and everything is going their way.

Sara sat on the stool in her footed pajamas and looked from one to the other as if sensing something was different this morning.

"Here, drink your orange juice," Danielle encouraged, setting the glass on the counter.

"Yes, ma'am," Kyle said, lifting his glass obediently.

Sara laughed and followed suit.

Her back to him, Danielle smiled, too. In spite of her worries, there was an inner clamoring to laugh, too, or to shout or to do something equally silly. Like go over and kiss her husband until they both melted.

"I'll walk Sara to school," he volunteered. "You stay inside. Are you going to work on the inventory today?"

"For most of the morning." Her voice broke and dropped to a hoarse whisper on the last word.

Sara giggled again. "Mommy sounds like a frog."

"Maybe she needs a prince to kiss her and turn her into a fairy princess," Kyle suggested.

The next thing Danielle knew, she was in his arms, being soundly kissed. It didn't last long, but it was thorough. Sara giggled the whole time.

"Nope, it didn't work," he said sadly. "She must not be a princess after all."

"Maybe you're not the prince," she retorted. The humor left his eyes instantly, and she was sorry for the remark.

"Maybe I'm not," he said on a light note. "Or maybe this gal is the magic princess." He blew raspberries against Sara's neck until her giggles drowned out the tension that had permeated the room.

Danielle poured the hot cereal into bowls and took them to the table, all the doubts about their future washing over her and depressing the foolish gaiety of the morning.

Later, after running a file merge between actual and supposed inventory, she saved the results and turned off the computer. She wandered through the house, sensing its emptiness as she went from room to room.

Coffee mug in hand, she sat on the sofa and let herself recall the events of the night. The hot, hot pleasure of their lovemaking. The wild ecstasy. The fulfillment.

And the need...the terrible, soul-wrenching need. Hers and his. Where would it lead them?

She stared out the window at the pine trees lining the drive. A man! Hiding in the trees!

Her heart raced like a runaway motor. The man moved, and she recognized him. It was Kyle.

Going to the window, she saw that he was removing the lower limbs on the trees up to head height. Then she realized why. It would be much harder to hide behind them and sneak up close to the house without the concealing lower branches. She sighed in relief.

Shortly before noon, he left in the truck and returned with Sara. They brought deli sandwiches, huge dill pickles and potato salad back with them.

"We're going to have a picnic," Sara announced. She led the way into the family room.

Kyle built a fire while Sara arranged the afghan on the floor and handed out the sandwiches. "Peter said he would beat up any bad men who came to our school. If he had a gun like Off'cer Rawlings, he would shoot 'em."

She was very pleased about this and had evidently put her faith into this new hero. Danielle smiled before biting into the hot meatball sandwich. Kyle had remembered her favorite. It's what she'd had their first meal together. That brought a warm, funny tingle to her heart.

"Guns are dangerous things," Kyle told their daughter. "A person has to be trained to use them very carefully. Like Officer Rawlings."

"Mommy has a gun."

"I went to the police shooting range. Jenny's dad taught me how to use it," Danielle quickly explained.

"Good." Kyle's eyes met hers. "I want you to carry it when you go out."

The old terror flooded through her. "Did you see anyone?" she asked, keeping her tone even.

Kyle shook his head. He'd seen an old pickup cruise the block a couple of times in the past few days. He'd seen it again on the road behind them yesterday. Nothing suspicious, but he'd had a gut feeling about it. He'd learned to go with his hunches in his years in undercover work.

He witnessed the fear return to Dani's eyes, but

otherwise she was calm and composed. Admiration grew in him. She had spunk, his woman. She hung in there when things got tough. It was a new facet, this leaner, meaner Dani.

"What are you smiling about?" she asked.

He grinned at her. "Remind me to tell you sometime. Maybe tonight."

A blush hit her cheeks. His grin broadened. She wasn't sure what to think about their lovemaking. Last night had been like the first time all over again, except he hadn't had to be quite as careful of her virgin sensibilities as he had six years ago.

He drew a careful breath as his chest filled with emotions he couldn't name. The one thing he was sure of—if Dani took him back, he would never leave his family again, job or no job. They were the important thing. He hoped it wasn't too late....

Danielle lay on the sofa while Sara talked to her friend Jenny on the phone. Kyle was back outside. He had half the trees trimmed and was working hard to finish them all before dark. She idly mused on the work he was doing around the house.

The new windows had made a big difference in the family room. He planned to do the kitchen next, then the bedrooms. He'd said he would finish them all that summer.

If he was there in the summer.

The doubt assailed her like a lead weight dropped on her chest, which still ached with every breath. A person would be foolish to trust too much.

In college she'd trusted a classmate, then had found he was dating her in order to get answers to some tests. He'd thought she would cheat for him. Although it hadn't been serious, being used had hurt. She'd learned to be cautious, which, she supposed, went with her quiet nature anyway.

With Kyle, everything had been different. She'd held back nothing, even though she'd known there was a part of him that was closed to her.

His work.

It had been the one off-limits subject. She had been so in love with him that she'd accepted his terms for their marriage without question. But when he'd disappeared for two years, she'd had to take a close look at her expectations of him, herself and their relationship.

She frowned and rubbed her aching temples. People changed. She'd been forced by circumstances to do so.

The question was the future. She would protect Sara with her life. Until this mess was over, Kyle would have to be part of their days. And their nights?

Shaking her head, she had to admit she didn't know. They would have to talk. He would have to commit to their future by giving his word to be there. Otherwise she didn't think she could take the uncertainty of never knowing when he would be gone and for how long.

There was a price for everything. That was hers for the future of their marriage.

Kyle knew at once that things had changed when he went in that night. He showered and changed into comfortable sweats before joining the girls in the kitchen. Danielle had all her defenses in place once more.

The pit of darkness shifted and roiled. Maybe he

had given up his rights to his family, but some stubborn part of him refused to accept that. He would have to tread carefully. He couldn't subdue Danielle in a show of force as if she were a criminal he was bringing down.

The fear that had haunted him for months and hit him full force when he'd read her letter concerning a divorce gnawed at him. In spite of last night he might not be able to bridge the chasm between them. But he had to try. He would use whatever he had—their passion, her generous heart, her concern, maybe even pity, for him.

And he was still Sara's father. That bond couldn't be severed. She would have to deal with him concerning their child. He would never give up his place in young Sara's life.

He watched Danielle move about the old-fashioned kitchen with that quiet, competent manner she had. His body stirred. He had this one advantage: together they created a fiery haven neither of them could resist. That and Sara were his strong suits. He'd play them for all they were worth.

"Ready?" she asked.

He nodded and rose to help her place the spaghetti and hot garlic bread on the table. He caught the scent of her shampoo and sweet essence and inhaled deeply. Peace filled his soul. Dani and Sara were his and be damned to anyone who tried to hurt them!

Chapter Eleven

By Friday, Danielle's cold was much better. The sore throat was gone, and she was left with only the sniffles. Her cold medicine took care of that.

Checking the calendar to make sure she didn't have any appointments she'd forgotten that weekend, she realized the first week of February had passed in a blink.

She had worked steadily on the library inventory all week and was ahead of schedule. She felt good about that. With one branch library and the book-mobile remaining, she would be done by the end of May at the latest. The summer would be free.

She paused and wondered what the rest of the year would hold. She had avoided thinking about the future all week.

Since Tuesday, she had shared Kyle's room. He

had made love to her in that tender, fierce way he had each night. It was as if they were newlyweds in some ways. In others, it wasn't. Sometimes she felt a part of her was missing....

Oddly, she wasn't sure if they were reconciled or not, or if he really was going to stay in Whitehorn.

She and Sara were. This was home now. She didn't plan on leaving. Not for a long time, if ever.

Hearing voices in the kitchen, she turned off the computer and stored the disks and file folders. Going into the other room, she found Shane McBride with Kyle.

"Hello," she responded to Shane's greeting and put on a fresh pot of coffee. She heated up the cinnamon biscuits she kept on hand during the cold winter months.

The men looked serious, she noted as she took a seat at the table. Alarm speared through her.

"You said you wanted to see me?" Shane began, glancing at Kyle.

Kyle nodded. "I wanted to know what precaution the sheriff's department has in place regarding your wife, safety-wise."

Shane's eyes narrowed. "Why?"

"I've been thinking about Sara and why the men are after her. That brings me to Angela."

Realization swept over Danielle. She laid a hand on his arm. "You think the men intend to kill both of them."

"Yes."

Shane's jaw looked as if it had been set in concrete. He muttered a curse. "No one is going to get to Angela. I have men watching her and the house during the day when I'm not home.''

"Put them on twenty-four hours a day," Kyle advised. "Tell them to be on their toes. I think things are coming to a head.''

"What makes you think so?" Shane asked, eyeing Kyle with a curious yet puzzled expression.

"First, there's a break in the weather and the roads are clear, so they'll be able to travel fast to get out of the area. Second, they need to get Sara out of the way. She's the only person who can identify them—''

"Other than Angela. She knows what Pierce looks like.''

"That's the third part of the equation. With Sara out of the way, that leaves only Angela. She has to tell them where the money is. Then they'll get rid of her. Or, if they decide she really doesn't know, they'll waste her and search the house for clues to the money. Either way, Angela loses.''

"And Sara," Danielle said, the stark terror of December and the kidnapping making her heart race.

"Exactly," Kyle agreed.

Shane glanced from one to the other. "Got any ideas?" he asked Kyle after a brief, assessing silence.

Kyle looked at Danielle. She sensed his reluctance to talk in front of her. She leveled a gaze at him and didn't look away. She could take whatever was to come, anything to protect their child. He nodded grimly.

"They'll have to make a move soon, before another storm heads in," he said, returning to Shane. "They want to get out of Whitehorn. Each day they hang around, it increases their chances of being caught in a snare.''

"You want increased surveillance here?''

"No. They're cruising the area. I think Pierce is smart enough to detect any cops hanging around disguised as telephone repairmen. They will have to make their move first. We'll have to be ready. Does your wife know how to handle a gun?''

"I don't think so.''

"You might take her to the police range and let her practice just in case it's a skill she'll need.''

"She's pregnant—''

"Do you think that will matter to Pierce?''

A dangerous fury flashed in Shane's eyes. "No.''

Danielle felt chills run over her scalp. They were such fierce warriors. Studying each of the men in turn, she recognized similar traits—a need to defend their homes, the will to protect their families, a determination that law and order would prevail.

But they weren't warriors all the time. Shane was all tenderness with Angela. And Kyle...

She recalled her husband's exquisitely gentle touches during the night. He'd kissed her a thousand times, a thousand different ways. And always there was that gentleness, even in the midst of the most explosive passion.

Their lovemaking was wonderful. She just didn't know what it meant to the rest of their lives.

She listened quietly while the other two discussed various scenarios for looking after their families. When Shane rose to leave, the men shook hands. Danielle saw the respect they had for each other. If Kyle stayed in the area, he would need a male friend, and he and Shane were close in age as well as experience.

"Why don't you and Angela come over for dinner tonight?" she invited. "While the roads are clear."

Shane smiled. "I'd like that. She's new here, you know, and doesn't know all that many people." He laughed briefly, grimly. "I think some people are afraid she might be dangerous to be around."

"The same as Sara," Danielle remarked with more than a smidgen of irony in her tone.

Kyle laid an arm over her shoulders. His touch told her he was there for her and Sara. She felt comforted.

"I'll check with Angela to be sure, but I don't recall any other plans. I'll let you know if we can't make it."

"Good. About seven then."

He nodded. Kyle walked with him to the door and returned. He stopped behind her chair and rubbed her neck and shoulders.

"It'll be okay," he murmured.

She sighed and leaned her head forward so he could massage all the achy muscles in her neck. "I want it to be over. I want Sara to be safe. I want..."

So many things. Once she'd thought all her dreams had come true. She'd met Kyle and life had been perfect. But now, the rosy tint had disappeared. Life was real. And it was harder than she'd ever imagined.

"My parents protected me from the world," she said.

"Not on purpose. They were college math professors. They still live in an ivy-covered tower."

Her folks, now retired from the Colorado University system, tutored part-time at a local community college. She loved them totally, but she had to admit Kyle was right. They lived in their own world, one that she had been a loving part of during her growing years.

"Do they still write you those funny letters?" he asked.

"Yes."

In the middle of telling her about some mundane happening in their lives, her parents, who jointly wrote her, would mention that they had found the most elegant little proof and would proceed to write it down. Or that so-and-so, a world famous mathematician who'd just won the Nobel prize or something, had dropped by and asked about her. If her parents had been disappointed in having a very ordinary daughter instead of a genius, they had never shown it in any way.

Kyle's youth had been very different from hers. She disliked his father, who was a grouchy, bitter old man who seemed to think life owed him something. She had always included him in her invitations for holiday meals, but he had never responded.

On a sympathetic impulse, she caught Kyle's hand and pressed kisses on the back of it.

"What was that for?" he asked, his smooth voice going deep and husky.

"For growing up to be a kind, caring, decent person."

He dropped to his haunches beside her chair and gazed into her eyes. "Don't feel sorry for me. That isn't what I want from you."

"What do you want?"

He frowned slightly as if the words were difficult

or he couldn't find the right ones. "You know," he finally said. Rising he went to the door. "I'll go pick up Sara. Stay away from the windows. You have your gun?"

"In the drawer."

"Wear it," he advised, his expression grim.

After he left, she tucked the .38 into her waistband. His worry over her and Sara was touching, she had to admit. He was a man to depend on in tough times.

But what about the rest of their lives? Would he find days of following the same routine boring? Some people got addicted to the adrenaline kick of danger. Would he wish he could leave?

If he did, she knew he would be too honorable to say so. She couldn't bear it if he was miserable while he lived in her quiet world.

She sighed shakily. They would have to discuss this. But not now. Later, when life was normal again.

"I can't believe there was ever a million dollars," Angela said, looking perplexed. "I mean, the business was bankrupt. I know. I had to pay off the creditors with what little I had. I sold everything that wasn't nailed down."

They were in the family room. Kyle had built a fire, and they were having dessert and coffee in there. Sara was in bed for the night.

"I, uh, had a friend do some checking," Kyle said. "He had an accountant go over the business accounts and compare the books to what the clients said they had paid. There was about a million missing."

Danielle was surprised at his hesitation. She was pretty sure the friend was Luke Mason, his contact with the FBI. They probably had access to records that Angela didn't.

"A million dollars," Angela repeated skeptically. "I can't believe it. Where would Tom have put it?"

"Did he have a girlfriend?" Kyle asked, his tone gentle as he brought the subject up.

"One?" Angela laughed without humor. "Many."

"Did the men in the parking lot use Tom's name when they demanded the money?" he continued.

Danielle glanced at Shane to see how he was taking Kyle's questioning of Angela. The lawman didn't appear offended, only deeply interested in the questions and the answers to them.

"Yes. I think so. Let me think." Angela closed her eyes and concentrated. "They had me trapped against my car. I was struggling to break free of them. Only one man spoke at that time. He used a rough whisper, as if he were hoarse. He asked me where the money was. I told him I didn't know anything about it."

"And then?" Kyle prodded.

"Well, that seemed to make him furious. He said he wanted the million dollars now and I'd better hand it over. I must have looked flabbergasted, which I was."

"But did he use Tom's name, or did he say your husband or something to indicate it could be Tom?"

Angela stared thoughtfully at Kyle. Finally she shook her head. "I'm sorry. I can't remember."

"Take your time," Shane encouraged.

"It was so frightening. The men wore ski masks. I'd never been robbed before. Then I heard screaming and saw the girls staring at us across the parking lot. One of the men released me and started after them. I tried to break free, but the other man, the one who had demanded the money, hit me.'' She touched a spot on her scalp. ''He had a gun.''

Kyle nodded grimly. ''And then you passed out?''

''Yes. When I came to, the police were there. Jenny was crying. Lynn was holding her. The men were gone.''

''With Sara,'' Kyle said grimly, ''thinking she was their ticket to another million dollars.''

Danielle relaxed when Kyle sat back on the sofa and heaved a deep breath. ''We were so lucky she got away,'' she said to Angela. ''She's talking again. Did Lynn tell you?''

''Yes. I was so relieved to hear it.''

''She's always been a chatterbox. Lynn and I would make a zip-your-lips motion to tell her she was talking too much. Today, when she came rambling on about her dog and what she was going to name it when she got one, I nearly motioned for her to zip it and then I realized what a contradiction that was to how I felt last week when she didn't speak.''

''I've often felt her being taken was my fault.''

''Not at all,'' Danielle hastened to assure the other woman. ''A person is responsible for his or her own actions. You couldn't possibly be blamed for what your former husband or those men did.''

''Some people aren't that understanding,'' Shane remarked. ''Some people in town think Angela knows something and isn't telling.''

''Oh, honestly.'' Danielle dismissed the narrow-minded busybodies with a quick toss of her head.

''What are the kidnappers going to do next?'' Angela demanded. "It's so frustrating, this not knowing."

Danielle stacked their used pie plates on a tray. "I know. Always being afraid each time you go outside. Being constantly alert for any strange sound. It's maddening."

"Don't drop your vigil," Shane said. "Willie, if he's in on this, might not be dangerous by himself, but the other guy is. He seems pretty ruthless."

"Money," Angela murmured. "A necessary evil."

Shane tousled her hair, his touch loving. "It's not always evil. I seem to recall you were pretty free with it when picking out baby furniture the other day."

That lightened the atmosphere. Angela's maternity top fluttered noticeably as the baby kicked. The four adults laughed.

"When is the baby due?" Danielle asked.

"In May. I can hardly wait. Shane has decided she's going to be a gymnast."

He patted his wife's tummy. "My daughter is going to the Olympics."

"He's going to adopt her," Angela said, looking at her husband with her heart in her eyes.

Danielle's breath caught in her throat at the tenderness between the other couple. "I could use a ton of money myself," she said, changing the subject. "This house is probably going to cost a fortune to renovate. But I fell in love with the site and the kitchen."

"I understand Kyle is real handy around the house," Angela said with a perfectly angelic expression on her face and an imp in her eyes. "Lily Mae Wheeler told me he was an expert on home repairs."

Kyle appealed to Shane. "Can't we lock that woman up on some charge for ten or twenty years?"

"Let me think on that. In the meantime, I have some repairs to do at our place. You interested in exchanging help on the big projects?"

"Sure."

The conversation turned to old houses and repairs and the men's plans for their respective places. Danielle joined Angela in teasing them unmercifully about the quality of their work.

"Well, one thing—we work cheap," Shane concluded.

Danielle laughed with the others. When the couple left, Kyle helped her clean up. She washed dishes while he dried.

"That was fun," he said after a comfortable silence. "Thanks for including me."

She looked a question at him.

"You don't have to," he said, his manner matter-of-fact, his eyes mysterious as he watched her. "Everyone knows our arrangement is temporary, only until we catch the men who took Sara."

"You said you were going to stay in the area. You may as well get to know some of the locals. You'll be working with Shane and Sterling and Rafe on other cases in the future, won't you?"

"That's right. I believe in the law enforcement agencies working together, rather than fighting each other."

"A good idea."

He smiled briefly.

"What?"

"You." He gazed into her eyes. "Just you."

Her heart speeded up. Sometimes, when he looked at her, it seemed as if all the gentleness in the world was gathered in his eyes, and then she felt she was the only woman in the world and that she mattered, really and truly, to him.

Her heart filled with yearning. If only they could go back and find whatever it was that had been lost.

He touched her temple. "It's all right," he murmured. "Don't worry so." He left to make his rounds.

After looking in on Sara, then getting ready for bed, she wondered at his words. Her mother had often said it didn't pay to worry about life, that whatever was going to happen would do so with or without a person giving herself a heart attack over it.

It was the uncertainty, she decided, that caused people to worry. Waiting for the kidnappers was like waiting for the other shoe to drop...only it felt like a guillotine was suspended over her head.

Kyle entered the truck stop out on the state highway. Two truckers sat at the counter. A rather scruffy-looking man sat in the booth near the front window. Kyle told the waitress he wanted coffee and went over to the booth.

"How's it going?" he said, taking a seat.

Luke Mason grinned at him from behind a week's growth of beard. He was dressed in ragged jeans and a thick sweater, a hole in one elbow, over a chambray shirt. "Things are fine from this end. How about yourself?"

"Nothing happening here on the kidnappers. It's driving me nuts." He sighed in disgust.

"Yeah, you always liked to be in the action." He eyed the undercover agent. "I put in the word for you to take over the field office here. You up to that?"

Kyle knew what his friend was asking. "I'm ready. Shuffling paper sounds pretty good after the last two years."

Luke studied him some more. "Something has changed. You're different, I think."

Kyle nodded. "I got my priorities straightened out."

"That letter from Danielle?"

"It…" He searched for words. "I made a decision concerning my family without giving them a say in it. Without even telling them what the decision was. That was stupid of me." He gave a snort of bitter laughter. "It taught me a lesson, one that isn't over yet."

"She going through with the divorce?"

Kyle flashed Luke a challenging glance. "Not if I can help it."

"Too bad. I always thought she was pretty special."

Kyle subdued the urge to sock his friend in the teeth. He knew Luke was ribbing him. He also knew his friend admired Danielle and thought he was damned lucky to have her. That had never been in question.

"What are you doing in these parts?" Kyle asked after his coffee had arrived and the waitress left.

"Well, now that my best undercover man is out to pasture, so to speak, I'm handling a couple of things on my own. We're shorthanded at the office. Did I tell you the old man had a heart attack?"

"No." Kyle was surprised. The agent they called the "old man" was older than the other men and had prided himself on staying in shape.

"Yep, right in the courthouse on the witness stand. He's going to be okay, but he's on R and R, too."

"Anything you need help on?" Kyle felt compelled to ask.

"No. You just take care of that sweet little family of yours." Luke sipped his coffee, then grinned over the rim of the cup. "It's good that you're keeping busy. I hear you're into home repairs these days."

Kyle groaned. "That story is going to haunt me the rest of my life. How the hell did you hear about it?"

"I was talking to a detective here, name of Sterling McCallum. You know him?"

Kyle nodded. "He's a good man."

"So are you," Luke said on a serious note. "You'll do a fine job in the field office here." He handed Kyle an envelope. "Congratulations. It's official."

Stunned, Kyle stared at the envelope as if it contained bad news, such as the one Luke had handed him from Danielle. He opened the letter and found the confirmation that he would be in charge of the local field office starting March 1.

As the local field director, he would assign agents to tasks great and small in a vast area. The FBI was spread rather thinly in the wide open spaces of the West.

"Do I still report to you?"

Luke shook his head and grinned. "I think you're one up on me now. You'll report straight to headquarters."

Kyle left the truck stop an hour later, his mind on

the upcoming job responsibilities. There was one
question on his mind. How would Dani see this
change?

His step quickened as he thought of home and family.

Chapter Twelve

Danielle entered the Hip Hop shortly before noon. The place was already crowded. She spotted Winona Cobbs at a table for two. The psychic waved her over.

"Join me," she invited. "I've been worried I was going to be without company this morning."

Her long gray hair was neatly braided into a coronet around her head, emphasizing her plump face and genial manner. Danielle liked the woman who was considered the local eccentric with her "visions" and the sort of glorified junkyard she owned.

"Thanks. I'm feeling rather lonely this afternoon. Sara is on a field trip with her class."

"She's doing well, I've heard." There was a question in Winona's tone.

"Yes." Danielle laughed softly as she picked up the menu and opened it. "I had vowed if she ever talked I was never going to tell her to shut up again. This morning at breakfast, she kept chattering while Kyle and I tried to discuss the day's plans. I drew a line across my mouth.'' She demonstrated. ''That's a signal she's talking too much and is supposed to zip it up. I couldn't believe I'd reverted to the 'children should be seen' scenario so soon.''

Winona's blue eyes crinkled in delight at the story. Her laughter made Danielle feel better.

''We are what we are,'' she said.

Danielle digested this remark. ''That sounds like one of those cryptic statements that leads to another.''

The seeress nodded. ''Your husband is a good man.''

The waitress came for her order before she could reply.

''You two have been in my thoughts lately. I've hesitated to say anything,'' Winona continued when they were alone. ''I didn't want you to think I was a nosy busybody.''

''I won't think that,'' Danielle promised. Her smile evaporated. ''I wish I knew what the future holds. For Kyle and me as a couple, for us as a family. We're in a kind of limbo at the present.''

Winona nodded solemnly. ''His is a protecting spirit. He will always be in law enforcement. If he tries to leave, his soul will wither away.''

Danielle listened attentively to the older woman. Whether she spoke from vibes or past experience or just common wisdom, her words made sense and affirmed much of what Danielle instinctively knew was true concerning her strong, silent husband.

''You will have to accept him as he is,'' the psychic continued after a pause, "or you will have to give up the marriage and him."

The pain speared deep into Danielle. She had known this, too, although she hadn't put it into words. "What about my needs? Don't they count for anything?"

Winona looked sympathetic, but didn't answer.

"It seems we must always consider the male's needs, but women are expected to ignore their own. Why? I want to be included in his life and in the decisions that affect us as a family. Is that too much to ask?"

"No," Winona agreed. "Have you told him?"

Danielle sighed, then smiled ruefully. "I've tried." She spread her hands. "I'm not a violet who will droop without daily attention, but he stayed away for two years. Two years without a word. He can't just walk back into my life, and Sara's, then be gone again."

"Ah," Winona said. "So that's the crux of it. Foolish on his part. He needs to find the courage to face his fear of something happening to you and young Sara."

"If we should die, you mean."

"Yes."

Danielle stared at the older woman. "I don't think I could bear it if he were killed. Or Sara."

"I think you could."

Winona took her hand in hers. Danielle felt the surprising strength in the older woman's touch. There was something very comforting in it. The psychic closed her eyes and sat very still.

"You have the strength to endure," she said after

a minute or so. "You held together during the time Sara was gone. You've been there for her since she returned. You are stronger than you ever imagined."

When she finished speaking, Winona sat back and dropped her hands in her lap. Danielle felt the loss of connection at once. Something about this old wise woman touched her and drew her into a shared web of experience.

The sisterhood of women, she mused. That common bond of womanhood, of being wives and mothers and the keepers of the light, part of something bigger that extended backward and forward into time and stretched outward to cover the world, crossing all barriers of age, race, money, beliefs.

"Sometimes I don't feel very strong," she admitted.

"We all feel that way at times. Even men."

Danielle's meal was delivered, but she hardly tasted it. While they talked of ordinary matters, her mind mulled over the past and the future. She had decisions to make and, she now realised, only she could make them.

Later, going to the grocery and running errands, she considered what those decisions should be. By the time she went to pick up Sara at school at three o'clock, she hadn't come to any conclusions.

After this is over, she promised, half listening to Sara's chatter about her field trip to the Indian museum, she and Kyle would talk. Together, she decided. They must decide together what each would give and what each would take and whether their marriage could work on that basis.

"We saw a million bones," Sara continued. "They

were from dead people who lived here a long time ago. You can tell lots of things from bones. One was a baby. And a skull of a girl Ms. Lynn said was six years old. It made me and Jenny sad. Why did she die?''

"She might have caught the flu," Danielle said. "They didn't have doctors like Dr. Carey back then. We're very lucky nowadays."

"Yeah. I like Dr. Carey. Except when she gives me a shot."

"The nurses usually give the shots."

"Yeah, but *she* tells 'em to."

Laughing, Danielle pulled into the garage. Kyle's truck wasn't there. She knew Luke Mason had called and talked to him the previous night. Another case?

Her blood chilled at the thought. "Come on, let's get the groceries and get inside."

They gathered an armload of bags. The wind blew fiercely as they crossed the path to the mudroom door.

"It's colder," she said, stopping to unlock the door. "There's a cold front moving in. We'll be getting more snow tomorrow probably."

"Oh, goody. School will be out. We can go sledding down the hill again, huh?"

Danielle shook her head. Sara was only in kindergarten and actually loved school, but she was already gleeful about snow days. By first grade, school would be passé, indeed. She pushed the door open with the toe of her boot and reached inside to turn off the alarm system.

"Hold it right there," a rough male voice commanded.

Danielle turned from the counter when she had deposited her groceries. Two men stood in the kitchen. She realized the outside door hadn't closed completely behind her.

Sara stood in the middle of the floor, her eyes huge and her hands pressed over her mouth. With the sickening sensation of falling in an elevator, Danielle realized she was face-to-face with the kidnappers. One of them held a gun pointed at her.

She didn't stop to think. With two running steps she was between Sara and the men. "Run, Sara! Run! Go to Jenny's house!"

Moving as she shouted, she lunged straight for the men, taking them by surprise. The smaller man stepped back, jostling the man with the gun and pushing them back into the mudroom.

"Run! Run! Run!" she screamed and plowed headfirst into the two men.

She grabbed their shirts up close to the throat and held on like a bulldog with a bone. Behind her, she heard a frightened squeal, then Sara's receding footsteps.

One of the men hit her arm. She nearly lost her grip. She wrenched back and forth on their shirts and brought her head up under the chin of the bigger guy. He cursed and beat at her back with the butt on his gun.

Hearing the slam of a door, she sagged in relief. Sara was out of the house. Now if she could just manage to hang on to the men and not get herself killed, help would come soon.

Using one foot, she hooked it behind the men's legs and yanked as hard as she could. They all went down in a heap in the small room. She heard thuds as her attacker's heads hit the washing machine on one side and the sink on the other. Both men cursed.

Grimly pleased, she wished the blows had knocked them out. No such luck.

Energy poured into her arms, and she struck out blindly, catching the smaller guy in the mouth. She felt the bite of his teeth into her knuckles, but the pain barely registered. She went for his eyes.

"Bitch," snarled the other man. "You'll pay for this."

She scrambled back from them, kicking with all her might to keep them distracted while she reached for her gun.

Point and fire.

She repeated the words in her mind like a mantra as she drew her weapon. At that moment, the bigger guy caught her ankle and shoved her leg aside. He threw himself across her. She heard the clunk of her gun as it hit the floor. Her arm was trapped under her. She couldn't move.

The kidnapper's eyes narrowed. "Get her gun," he ordered the smaller man.

"What gun?"

"The one she has behind her."

His breath touched her face. His eyes showed no mercy, only a maddened hatred at being thwarted. She heaved her head forward and hit him on the chin.

"You…"

That was the last she heard. His gun crashed into her temple and the world blinked out.

"She's here somewhere."

Danielle heard the words from a distance. Her mind

was strangely groggy. Opening her eyes and looking around wildly, she realized she couldn't move. A piece of tape covered her mouth. Her arms were taped behind her, her ankles to the legs of a kitchen chair. She glanced around fearfully. Sara was nowhere in sight. That was good.

She glanced at the clock on the stove. She'd only been out a few minutes. She prayed Sara was safely at Jenny's house and Jenny's dad was busy rounding up some cops to come to her rescue. She wondered why she was still alive.

"We've got to find the kid."

"Hell, Dillon, she ran off," the smaller man said. "She's probably halfway to McCallum's house by now."

The man called Dillon smiled. "She's here. Kids don't run far from their mommas."

"I heard the door slam," Willie insisted.

"It wasn't an outside door," Dillon said, his eyes on her. "We would have felt the air flow if it had been."

Despair filled her. He was right. Cold air would have flowed into the house and sucked at the ill-fitting back door. Where had Sara gone?

Keeping an eye on them, she began to work the tape loose from her mouth, using her tongue to moisten it so it wouldn't stick. She worked on her wrists, too, and found the tape loosening somewhat. Each time one of the men glanced at her, she held still, her heart thudding so hard she marveled that they didn't hear it.

Another odd thing—she wasn't afraid. After the

first shock of seeing them and her fear for Sara, it was as if she had accepted the worst: they would kill her—and it no longer had the power to terrify.

"Go look for the kid," Dillon ordered.

"Where?"

Danielle didn't miss the resentful tone. Neither did his partner.

Dillon shot the other man a withering glance. "In her room. In closets. Under the bed. Didn't you ever play hide-and-seek when you were a kid?"

"No," Willie said sullenly. He walked into the hall.

Danielle heard his footsteps in the family room. Attuned to every nuance, she followed his progress from room to room. She heard the opening and closing of closet doors, the screech of furniture as he moved things out of the way. Every muscle in her body was frozen in dread of hearing Sara's cry of terror or his of triumph if he found her.

Finally, after twenty minutes, he returned. "She ain't in the house," he announced.

"Hell," Dillon said. "Do I have to do everything myself?" He got up and came to her.

With a snatch that nearly ripped the skin off her face, he removed the tape from her mouth.

"Where is she?"

Danielle stared at him without answering.

He slapped her, then leaned close. "If you want to live to see sundown, you'd better tell us where she hid."

Danielle gave a snort of laugher. "I don't know where she might hide. Neither would I tell you if I did—"

Ring. Ring.

The three of them jerked around as if controlled by a single puppet string. The phone rang again.

"You expecting anybody?" Dillon asked.

"Yes," she lied. "An officer from the sheriff's department is supposed to come over."

Dillon stared at her for a long moment. "You're lying." He turned to Willie. "Come on. We'll both look. Did you go upstairs?"

"Uh, no," Willie admitted. "I don't think a kid would go up there. It's dark and cold."

Dillon laughed cruelly. "You big chicken," he scoffed. "Come on. This time we're going to look in every room." He led the way into the hall.

Please, oh, please, she silently prayed. *Please don't let them find Sara.*

She couldn't figure out if her daughter had actually made it out of the house. Her spirits lightened. Maybe Sara had gotten away. Maybe she was on her way to Jenny's house right now.

Reality returned with a thump as she heard furniture being overturned in one of the bedrooms. A crash indicated her office had been invaded. Dillon was trashing the place while he searched.

She realized she had never come upon a truly ruthless, uncaring person before. Dillon had no compassion in him. She saw that in the flat, opaque glare of his eyes. He cared nothing for anyone or anything, a man without a soul.

These were the type of men Kyle dealt with constantly in his job. These men were the ones he fought to bring to justice day after day. Sometimes the courts set them free on a technicality after Kyle and his coworkers had risked their lives—and sometimes lost them—in making the arrest. How did he stand it year after year?

And how, she wondered, did he maintain that core of gentleness he showed to her and Sara when he had to deal with such men as these?

Listening to sounds of destruction as the men searched the attic rooms over her head, she struggled with the tape securing her wrists, the anger growing in her by the minute.

Kyle looked the neighborhood over as usual as he drove home. He slowed at a spot where he could see through the trees and checked the front of the house. Nothing unusual.

Driving past the street, he turned up the road that ran in back of the house and the empty field behind it. All calm there. Light glowed in the kitchen window as the shadows of twilight deepened.

The house beckoned him. It signaled warmth and human companionship. Sara and her chatter. And Dani.

He could no more resist the pull of her than the ocean could resist the pull of the moon. Every bit of feeling in him surged in a tidal wave of need toward her. She was the light that shone into the darkest reaches of his soul and kept him sane in a crazy world. She was the peace that made the worst nightmare bearable.

Living through the hell of worrying about Sara and her all the time forced him to see, up close, something of what she went through when he was on a case. He'd put her through two years of that.

When this was over, he'd get out of her life. If that was what she wanted. The dark pool bubbled and roiled, as if it waited to suck in his soul.

He would have to learn to live without her. He would have to watch her fall in love and marry another man…have his children…build a new life.…

Slowing to a crawl, he stared hungrily at the house, wanting a glimpse of her as she bustled about the kitchen. She would be fixing dinner. Sara would be on the stool, talking up a storm now that she wasn't afraid to speak.

He peered at the house, but couldn't detect anyone moving around. There was a stillness about the place that prickled the hair at the back of his neck. His cell phone rang at that moment.

"Mitchell here," he answered.

"Kyle, Shane. We just got a call on 911 from your place. Sara says the bad men have her mom. She's hiding. The men are looking for her. It must be the kidnappers. I'm on my way in an unmarked car. Rawlings and McCallum are, too. Cruisers are moving into position to block every street in the area."

A howl of pain and rage echoed through his mind. Then it was gone. "Right. I'm on the road behind the house. Hold on and I'll check the place where they hid their truck when they came to the house before."

He drove on down the county road.

"Yeah, it's here." He gave the make, model and year of the pickup as well as the license number. "I'll block it in, then I'm heading for the house."

"Right. We'll be there as soon as the rest of the men are in place and the roads blocked."

Kyle rang off and pulled in close behind the

pickup. After letting the air out of its back tires, he headed for the house, keeping the garage between him and the house. The kidnappers had done the same thing. He walked in their prints until he reached the converted stables.

He checked the round of ammunition in his gun, then eased around the garage. Bending below the window level, he dashed for the house. He waited, listening.

There was no sound other than the wind through the trees. He wondered what had happened to the alarm. The remote receiver in the truck should have gone off when the men broke in. Unless they came in on Danielle after she was home and had turned it off.

She was valiant. She must have fought with them while Sara got away. One person didn't have much chance against two. She might be lying unconscious on the floor. She could be bleeding…shot….

He slammed the door on the worry. He couldn't afford to be distracted. Too much was at stake.

At the back door, he paused and listened. Still nothing. He eased the door open. Nothing.

He slid inside and silently closed the door. Weapon ready, he peered around the door frame.

Relief poured through him. Danielle sat with her back to him. She was working at the masking tape wrapped around her wrists.

"Dani," he said quietly.

Her head whipped around. Her eyes widened. His name formed on her lips, but she uttered no sound. He put a finger to his mouth, then headed toward the hall.

"They're upstairs, looking for Sara," she whispered.

They heard a crash and footsteps in the attic. The men must be searching through the odds and ends stored up there for Sara.

He turned back to quietly free Danielle before he went upstairs after the men. He holstered his gun and removed his pocket knife. Flicking a blade out, he reached for her bound wrists. She twisted around to watch.

"Be still," he cautioned. "They taped you up pretty good. I'm going to have to go under the—"

He got no further. He heard a startled cry from Danielle then felt a shattering blow to the back of his head. He fought his way back from the brink of darkness.

He rose and turned at the same time, bringing his fist up and driving it with all his might into his assailant. The breath rushed out of the man as he caught the kidnapper in midsection. Unfortunately the blow didn't lay him out.

They grappled and rolled to the floor, each trying to get a paralyzing hold on the other. They were evenly matched. Kyle, his vision occasionally blurring, managed to keep a hold on the man's wrist and the gun pointed upward as they struggled.

"Back off," another male ordered. "I'm gonna shoot."

Kyle spared a glance at the new threat. The other kidnapper stood in the doorway, waving a gun at them. He winced as he took a blow to his rib cage, but he didn't let go of his assailant. The struggle intensified as the crook realized his partner was there to help.

Danielle stared in horror at the men on the floor. Kyle, blood running down his forehead, wrestled fiercely with Dillon, neither able to get the upper hand. Willie, pointing *his* gun at the men, shifted from one foot to the other in uncertainty.

"Back off," Willie ordered, pointing the gun at Kyle.

The men on the floor ignored him.

She strained against the tape binding her hands but it was useless. She couldn't break fee.

Please, oh, please, she said over and over, a litany begging for help, praying for his safety. Even if Kyle overpowered Dillon, Willie still had the gun. Given the desperate expression on his face, he might use it.

She struggled mightily and found she could lift the chair off the floor by throwing herself forward. That didn't help that she could see. She couldn't hop away, carrying the chair like a hermit crab searching for a safer place.

Oh, please.

At that moment, Kyle rolled on top. He held Dillon down and repeatedly smacked his hand against the floor until Dillon lost his grip and dropped the gun. Kyle knocked the weapon across the room. It skittered out of sight between the wall and the trash can.

Raising his arm, he drew back his fist, his left hand holding Dillon by the throat.

"Get off him or I'll shoot," Willie shouted.

Danielle stared at the men. Willie's eyes held the wild look of a cornered beast. Fear scalded her heart. He was going to shoot.

She lunged forward until she was on her feet, the chair legs off the floor. Then as Willie screwed one eye closed and took aim, she threw herself headlong into him, taking him by surprise.

The gun went off at the same moment they went down in a heap. The noise was so loud, her ears rang and all other sounds receded into the distance, as if she were underwater.

A second or an eternity went by.

Willie tried to push her aside. She kept all her weight centered in his chest. With a final heave, he shoved her off him. She teetered on two legs of the chair, then fell in a heap on her side, whacking her head on the floor.

"My God, he's dead," Willie said, horror in his voice. "I shot his face clean off." He fainted.

Danielle tried to see, but Willie blocked her view. She could hear Willie breathing in gasps. And one other man.

She closed her eyes and gave a low moan of despair. "No," she said. "No, no, no..."

Chapter Thirteen

The back door burst open. "Police! Don't anyone move!"

Danielle identified Rafe Rawlings as he entered the kitchen from the mudroom. Three other officers were behind him.

"Looks like we got here too late," she heard Shane McBride say in a quiet tone. "Danielle, you okay?"

She felt hands at her wrists and others at her ankles. "Yes, I'm fine. Please. See about Kyle. He's hurt. Call an ambulance. Please."

Please don't let him be dead. Dear God, please..."

"Please—"

"Dani, it's okay," a soft masculine voice assured her. "I'm okay. It was Dillon who was shot."

His face came into view. One eye was swollen almost shut. Blood followed several paths down his forehead and temple and was smeared across the right side of his face. He had never looked so handsome.

"I thought…" she began, then had to stop. She swallowed. "I thought…"

"Shh. I know. It's okay."

Her hands and feet were free. She sprang up from the floor and the overturned chair. Kyle crushed her in his arms. Willie stirred and groaned. Rafe hooked the man's wrists at his back with handcuffs.

She got a glimpse of Dillon Pierce, lying on the floor. Blood covered half his face. The other half looked peaceful and serene, as if he merely napped.

Kyle turned her from the scene and pressed her face into his shoulder. "It isn't a pretty sight."

"I know." She sighed shakily and wrapped her arms around his waist and held on. Her legs were trembling, causing tremors to race up her body in waves. "You're hurt," she said, tasting blood when she licked her lips.

"It's nothing."

"Okay, we're clear here," Shane said into his radio. "Yeah, we need an ambulance. No need to hurry, though. Yeah, it's Dillon Pierce." He looked over at her for confirmation.

She nodded. "Dillon Pierce and Willie Sparks. You were right," she said to Kyle. "They wanted Sara—" Her breath was wrenched away. She pulled back from Kyle. "Sara! We've got to find her—"

Kyle caught her hand. "I think I know where she is. Come on." He glanced at Shane, who nodded.

Together she and Kyle walked down the hall and into her office. Her heart skipped a beat when she saw the mess. Her computer and the monitor were smashed. An old ornate gilt mirror hanging over a bricked-up fireplace was on the floor, the mottled mirror cracked into a spiderweb of lines.

Kyle set her chair upright and moved it out of the way. He closed the drawers on the desk and shoved it aside, then he knelt and opened a tiny door in the side of the old fireplace. Sara sat huddled in a little ball. She blinked up at them, her eyes wide with worry.

"Mommy? Daddy?" she said. "Are we safe yet?"

"Yeah, punkin, we're safe," Kyle told her and lifted her into his arms. The portable telephone dropped to the floor. He replaced it in its cradle, then he reached for Danielle and included her in a warm, heartfelt and very gentle bear hug.

"I did like you said," Sara told them. "I hid." She paused and looked ashamed. "But I forgot to call until I heard the phone ring."

"But you did call," Kyle reminded her.

"Yeah, but not till later. Willie and Dillon were in here so I couldn't come out. When I heard them upstairs, I comed…came out and got the telephone, then went back into the little closet."

The "little closet" had been used to store firewood in the days before the fireplace had been bricked up. Danielle recalled seeing it when they moved in, then she'd forgotten about it because the desk blocked the small door from view.

"You did exactly right," Kyle assured his daughter. With an arm around Danielle, he led the way back to the others, but steered them away from the kitchen and into the family room. "Stay in here," he told

Danielle, placing Sara in her arms. "Until things are cleaned up."

She thought of the kitchen and Dillon and the smear of blood on the floor where it had run down his neck. She wondered if the spot would ever come out. Or if it did, would she always see it there anyway, a grim reminder of this day of death and terror?

"That must be the ambulance," he murmured when they heard a siren.

With a pat on her shoulder, he strode out. She sat in the recliner and held Sara, who had fallen silent and lay with her head on Danielle's breast as if she were tired from a hard day at play.

"Will Willie go to jail?" Sara asked at one point when they saw Willie being taken away in a police cruiser.

"Yes. It's a very bad thing to kidnap people or break in someone's home and scare them."

"Were you scared?"

"Very much."

Sara sat up and looked at her. "You grabbed Dillon and Willie and held on, even when Dillon hit you with the gun."

That explained why her back ached in peculiar places. Also her head. Danielle didn't recall feeling the blows when they were delivered. All her efforts had been on holding the men until Sara got away.

"A person does what she has to," she said and smiled at Sara, not to make light of the incident, but determined that it wasn't going to haunt her or her daughter's life. "I'm glad that you hid. Dillon would have caught up with you before you could get to Jenny's."

"Daddy told me what to do. We practiced every day. Only I forgot the phone." She was crestfallen.

"But you remembered later," Danielle assured her. "And then you were very careful to make sure Dillon and Willie were someplace else before you came out. That was very smart. Daddy and I are very proud of you."

From the window, Danielle saw the ambulance leave after the medics had examined her, Kyle and Sara. The rumble of men's voices in the kitchen and outside grew quieter. The patrol cars also left. A few minutes later, Kyle entered the family room.

"How about a pot of coffee?" he asked.

Danielle nodded. He took Sara from her. The three of them went to the kitchen. All traces of Dillon and the blood were gone. She cast Kyle a grateful glance, knowing he had done it. She put the coffee on and heated the rest of the coffee cake.

Standing at the sink, she saw Rafe Rawlings and a couple of other men stringing crime tape and going over the grounds. On the street she saw a reporter from the local paper calling questions to Rafe and taking notes. While she watched, a van with an antenna drove up. A man with a camera hopped out the back and started shooting pictures of the house and the policemen in the yard.

"There's a television van here," she said.

"I suspect we'll be on the national news tonight," Kyle told her. He put Sara on her stool and took his seat.

"Well, all in a day's work," Shane said, entering

from the back door. He tossed a wry grin at Kyle's battered face. "You'll be real pretty in technicolor."

Danielle had prepared an ice pack. She brought it over to him. "Let me see."

He sat still while she gently put the bag of ice on it. He held it in place while she served the coffee and cake.

When she sat down, he reached over and touched her face. She winced a little, realizing she had a bruise there.

"Dillon?" Kyle asked.

"Oh, yes. He slapped me when I wouldn't tell him where Sara might have hidden. Thank you for practicing with her. It probably saved her life."

An expression both fierce and tender came into his eyes. "You saved her life," he corrected softly.

Warmth seeped into her and the last of the tremors subsided. She sighed and took a drink of coffee. It really was over. At last. Suddenly she wanted to lay her head on the table and bawl her eyes out.

Nerves. The fears of the last couple of hours, and months, catching up with her. She understood that. She willed the tears away.

"We'll need a statement from you and Miss Sara, the heroine here," Shane said to Danielle.

"I'm a fairy princess," Sara told them, her small face very earnest. "I pretended the mean ol' witch had put me in a magic cave and I couldn't get out until the prince came and broke the evil spell." She smiled at her father. "Just like you told me in the story."

"That's right." Kyle tousled her hair. "You're a

perfect princess. The spell is broken and the bad men are gone. Forever.''

Shane got a call from Sterling. When he hung up, he grimaced in disgust, then said sympathetically. ''The press is clamoring for the story. Are you three up to a statement? We'll keep it brief, just that the men broke in and held Danielle and Sara hostage, that Sara here called 911 and saved the day.'' He grinned and tweaked Sara on the nose.

Kyle gave her a questioning look. She nodded. The sooner they got it all done, the sooner they could be alone. She swallowed against the knot in her throat. No hysterics now, she sternly ordered. It's over.

''We'll need a statement at headquarters, too. Sterling said tomorrow was soon enough for that.''

''Good.'' Kyle stood. ''Let's talk to the reporters, then we'll clean up the mess. Your office is pretty bad. I doubt if we can salvage anything.''

''I know. The inventory files are current, so I'm okay there. I can use a computer at the library to finish.''

''We'll get you a new one,'' he declared firmly. ''We'll see how good that homeowner's insurance policy is.''

They had a brief stint in front of the cameras—by now there were three vans in front of the house and a half dozen stringers for various newspapers around the country. A report had already gone out on the wire services from the first guys on the scene, she learned.

''It'll be a three-day wonder,'' Kyle murmured to her as they returned to the house with questions still being fielded by Shane.

Rafe was in the kitchen with a camera crew. He'd

let them film a brief on the wrecked office and in the kitchen. When they entered, he made the crew leave the house.

"I've called a tow truck. We're impounding Willie's pickup. You want me to bring yours around to the garage here?"

Kyle nodded and tossed Rafe the keys to his pickup, which was blocking Willie's truck. "Thanks."

Rafe flashed him a sympathetic smile in that silent communication of men and headed out. The house was quiet once more.

"I need to call Luke," Kyle said.

Danielle nodded. "I'm going to straighten up."

She and Sara started in the bedrooms. Kyle joined them in a few minutes. In a little over an hour, they were finished downstairs. Her office was the worst room. Kyle carted the trashed electronic devices to the garage for later disposal.

Upstairs, the men had gone through some old trunks in the attic and had tossed aside several boxes Danielle hadn't gotten around to unpacking. Kyle stacked the boxes neatly while she and Sara threw old clothes and newspapers in garbage bags. Sara found a long dress, its white lace yellowed with age and smelly with mildew, and immediately had to put it on and see how she looked. She ran downstairs to the bathroom mirror.

"I've been meaning to clean these out," Danielle remarked to Kyle, gesturing toward the trunks. "The museum might be interested in some of the clothing. I want to refurbish the trunks and use them downstairs for storage and conversation pieces."

"Good idea," Kyle said absently.

He had stopped replacing items in one of the boxes that had broken open and was studying something, his face a mask of intense concentration. She went over to see what he had found that was so engrossing.

"Oh," she said, seeing the album in his hands.

"Our wedding pictures."

She stared at the pictures. She looked unbelievably young and naive, staring up at her handsome, serious and very new husband as if he were the sun and moon and stars wrapped in one.

Six years and two months ago.

She'd been a December bride. Her dress was a soft wool in winter white. He'd worn a dark suit. Her corsage of pink roses had been a gift from him, a thoughtful surprise. He'd worn a boutonniere of one pink rose.

It had been a quiet wedding in the minister's office. Danielle had brought her camera and the minister's wife had taken the pictures for them. They had eaten dinner with wine and candlelight at an expensive restaurant. Then they had returned to their small house.

"It seems so long ago," she murmured. "I'd wondered where the pictures were. I couldn't find them—"

She stopped abruptly as emotions she'd carefully locked away in a small hidden place inside her rushed out like the unbound spirits of Hallow's Eve.

His eyes met hers.

"It was a long time ago," he said softly. "A lifetime."

She couldn't read anything in his gaze other than a quiet intensity that spoke to her of sadness, a remorse for things past. She wondered if he regretted the marriage, knowing now that he should never have committed himself to that final step.

Turning away, she gathered the bags and tossed them down the stairs, one at a time.

"I'll take those to the garage," he volunteered, still holding the album, that same quiet expression on his face.

"Thanks. I think I'll take a hot shower and change before starting dinner." She managed a smile. "I ache in some odd places. You probably do, too. I won't be long in the shower," she promised.

Once in the bathroom with the door safely closed—there was no key for the old-fashioned lock—she turned the water on full force, then stripped and climbed into the tub.

For a minute she stood there with her eyes closed and let the water cascade down her back. She swallowed and cleared her throat. She tried not to think, not to let the sadness overwhelm her. Finally she rested her arms against the tiles and hid her face in the crook of her elbow.

The tears came.

Once started, she couldn't stop them. She cried for all the dreams she'd once had, for the love that had built and built inside her, for all the tenderness that couldn't be shared because the person it belonged to had left.

She cried for Sara and all the frightened days and nights the child had spent while kidnapped. She cried for herself and those same terrible days and nights of being alone and in terror for her child.

She cried for all the sweet tender moments of the

past and for all the ones that wouldn't be part of their future.

And most of all, she cried for them as a family, for the memories they would always have, for the times she and Kyle would meet as strangers who had shared an intimate and passionate past...at Sara's graduation, at her marriage, at the birth of their grandchildren.

"Dani, don't," she heard Kyle say.

She felt his hands on her shoulders, then the touch of his body as he turned her and held her. She tried to stop, to control the rush of tears, but they seemed to come from a bottomless well.

"Shh," Kyle said, soothing her as he would young Sara. Worry ate at him. He'd never heard Dani cry like this. She got teary-eyed in movies, but he'd never heard her sob, had never felt her body shake. "Don't cry. It's okay. It's okay now. It's over."

"I cuh-cuh-can't stuh-stop," she said. She hid her face in her hands, as if embarrassed for him to see her tears.

"Okay, I can handle that." Quietly stripping out of his now damp clothes he stepped into the tub with her and pulled her closer into his embrace, pressing her face against his chest. He rubbed the back of her neck and discovered a lump where she'd been struck. "Cry then. I'll hold you until it's over."

She kept her hands over her face as she wept. The water hit his head and shoulders, splashed over them. Her grief seemed endless, more than an emotional release from the terror of the attack. He worried about that, about this sorrow that seemed drawn from her soul. The dark pit of his soul churned restlessly.

But no expression of grief, no matter how deep,

can last forever. When she finally quieted, he lathered his hands and gently washed her. He shampooed her hair and recalled how he'd once loved to do that. Her hair was like holding dark flames in his hands. They had taken all their showers together early in their marriage.

When had he let the wonder go out of their marriage?

By the time he rinsed them both, the water was rapidly turning cold. He turned the faucets off and urged her from the tub. She looked so weary and she stood quietly and let him rub her dry. Her eyes were downcast, and she never once looked his way.

Goose bumps swept over them both when he led the way across the hall and into the bedroom. He held her nightgown while she slipped it on, then he buttoned it all the way down. When he was dressed in clean sweats, he took Dani's arm and ushered her toward the family room.

Sara was in her room, wearing a pair of Dani's high heels and holding a pink-and-gold magic wand in her hand when he looked in on her. She was singing a song. He sighed in relief. Their daughter was going to be fine.

Once he had Dani on the sofa, he built a fire, then turned to study her face. She looked drained.

The way he felt. It was the usual aftermath of intense strain, he could have told her. The danger and emotional shock of death and all that went with it took its toll on a person.

He'd been lucky. He'd had her to come home to. She'd been his light, his guide out of the darkness.

She'd filled his soul with warmth and given him peace.

What had he ever given her in return?

Danielle rinsed the mop and stored it in the mudroom. The house was clean, really clean, once more. Over the weekend and most of the week, there had been a steady parade of law enforcement officials and reporters, and a few friends who dared brave the mob, in and out of the house, tracking mud and snow all over.

Sara had gotten quite used to being the star of television and radio until she and Kyle had put their collective foot down on any more interviews. The latest thing—and she still didn't believe it—was the President, yes, *the* President, wanted to give her some kind of award for her quick thinking, according to someone who'd called an hour ago. Someone also wanted to use Sara in an ad in which various serious scenes were enacted—fire, unconscious adult—while Sara advised kids to call 911 for help when trouble brewed.

Danielle wanted to help other families, but she wasn't sure about the added publicity. She'd had enough and wanted life to go back to normal.

Right. Like the past two years?

After removing a pan of brownies from the oven, she sat at the table and mused on the week's events. Then her mind drifted into a hazy state where she didn't think at all. She liked that best. Life was easier if she didn't think.

Hearing Kyle's truck in the drive, she roused herself and cut the brownies, then stored half in a plastic bag and half in the cookie jar. She put the brownies in a bag she'd packed along with a wrapped present.

Sara had wanted Danielle to sleep in her room after the bout with the kidnappers. She had moved back to the big bed in there for the past few nights. Kyle had stayed in the master suite. Tonight Sara was spending the night with Jenny and they were going to a birthday party the next day. Jessica had suggested it as a way to get the girls' lives back on a normal track after the tensions of December and January.

Danielle glanced at the calendar. Saturday, February the thirteenth. She smiled slightly. If the date had been Friday, the thirteenth, she would have insisted that Sara stay locked in the house with her all day. She didn't want to tempt fate into sending more bad luck.

"Mommy, we're home," Sara called out, rushing into the house ahead of her father. "It's snowing. We have to hurry."

Danielle interpreted that to mean Sara was anxious to get to Jenny's before the roads closed. One learned early to be aware of the weather in Montana. Sara was excited about visiting her friend. There was a surprise waiting for her at Jenny's, too.

Wayne Kincaid had cleared it beforehand. He and his wife, Carey, were having dinner with the Mc-Callums. They were going to bring the female puppy for Sara and give it to her there. Jenny was so excited she could hardly stand keeping the secret.

Such good friends. Tears suddenly filled Danielle's eyes. She blinked in embarrassment.

Kyle followed his daughter in, closing the door behind them. He stored the milk in the fridge.

"Ready?" Kyle asked.

His face was flushed from the cold. His eyes were the deep-blue of mountain lakes in the summer. Her gaze locked with his for the briefest instant. She looked quickly away.

"Yes. I have Sara's bag packed. There are brownies inside, so don't toss it around," she warned Sara.

"Oh, yum," Sara exclaimed.

Danielle envied her daughter's ability to seemingly bounce back to normal. She still felt drained inside. She had a strange ache in her heart, too, as if some unseen weight rested there, pulling her down....

"How about we go out to dinner after we get rid of the pest here?" Kyle suggested.

"I'm not a pest," Sara told him, not the least indignant or offended. "I'm a hero."

"And you haven't heard the latest," Danielle murmured to Kyle when Sara pranced off toward the door, her duffel bag banging along the floor.

"Be ready when I get back." There was a question in Kyle's voice.

She nodded. Going out to dinner sounded like a good idea. They wouldn't be alone in the house. Until later.

Watching the other two leave, she considered her decision. She wasn't going to move into the master bedroom with Kyle. The danger was over. It was time for him to go.

She was giving him up.

He would grow to hate the desk job. And then he would grow to hate her for holding him back. She had thought it all out. Now all she had to do was carry through.

The heaviness beat at her. She would learn to live with it. Maybe it would grow lighter with time.

She went to the bedroom and pulled out a pair of flannel slacks and tossed them on the bed. A pair of black knit, clingy leggings caught her eye. She hesitated, then removed them from the hanger and put the flannels away.

After selecting a black sweater and a thigh-length jacket with black and gold threads, she showered and dressed quickly, aware of time passing.

She blow-dried her hair and added a few touches of makeup, plus the gold earrings and a chain that had been her first Christmas present from him. She'd just stepped into dressy loafers when she heard Kyle enter the kitchen.

"I'm ready," she called.

His smile was quick, but solemn as he looked her over. "That's one thing I always liked about you— you never keep a man waiting."

"Or a woman," she told him. "My mother said it was a courtesy from kings and a necessity from everyone else."

He led the way to the truck which he'd left near the door, engine running. "It's getting colder. We're supposed to get another ten to twelve inches of snow tonight."

"And there's another front behind this one."

"We'll be snowed in until the end of June this year if this keeps up."

She thought of a long winter snowed in with him, just the two of them in a cabin far removed from the rest of the world. A foolish fantasy. She'd never had him to herself like that. She'd never asked for or expected it. All she'd wanted was....

His love?

His undying devotion?

No, his presence. At fairly regular intervals. He couldn't give her that, and she couldn't live in the lonely marriage of the past two years.

So she would let him go.

Instead of taking her to the local diner, he drove out to the highway where more upscale establishments catered to the tourists as they left Yellowstone. He wheeled into the lot of an expensive steak-and-seafood house and parked. The sign out front said there would be dancing with a live band at nine o'clock.

Nine. Huh. With a five-year-old getting up at the crack of dawn, nine was close to her bedtime these days. She smiled faintly.

"What?" he asked. He leaned across and opened the door for her.

"Sara. She's going to be so excited about the puppy. She and Jenny will talk half the night, then get up at dawn. I'm glad Jessica has them and I can sleep in."

He paused before removing his arm from across her. His mouth was close to hers, his eyes near enough that she could see the dark-blue outer circle and the lighter shade near the pupil. "You could use the rest," was all he said.

Before she'd hardly slid out, he was there, his arm extended. She tucked her hand into the crook of his elbow and let him lead her inside.

The restaurant was dark and intimate. Candlelight

gleamed on pale-green linen and real silverware. The host seated them in a snug corner near the fireplace. Kyle ordered kir royales—a concoction of champagne and fruit liqueur—for each of them. She'd first had them on her wedding night.

A fitting goodbye—candlelight and champagne, all done with quiet elegance and style.

The ache in her chest intensified.

Their dinner was leisurely. She enjoyed it to the fullest—as if she were a prisoner at her last meal. As the evening flitted by, her eyes were drawn more and more to him. She couldn't look away. She wanted to devour him with her gaze until every nuance of his was a part of her.

Their last date. She wanted to remember it.

The music changed. Glancing around she saw a small combo on the stage. The leader introduced the men while they kept up a steady throbbing tempo of chords. They started with a fast tune.

"Come on," Kyle said. "You always liked to dance."

"All societies do," she informed him. "There's something about music and rhythm that appeals to all people in all parts of the world." Then she was embarrassed at how like a librarian she sounded.

He grinned at her and she felt heat rush to her face.

She hesitated, but he was already on his feet, his hand out to her. She joined him, but she was worried. It didn't seem wise.

But the beat was engaging and worry faded as they twisted and twirled. Kyle's dancing was as good as his singing. He had a natural grace on the dance floor that brought more than one envious glance her way.

The music changed to a slow beat without a stop. For a second she worried, but when Kyle took her in his arms, his hold was casual, not sexy at all.

She relaxed and let the music take her.

Gradually, the light dimmed even more and spotlights threw rotating multicolored beams of light over the floor. And somehow she was cuddled against his chest, his chin touching her forehead lightly. She wondered if this was wise and lifted her head to gaze at him.

The tables had turned, she realized, her breath catching in her throat. His eyes devoured her.

She couldn't look away. In those fathomless depths were every dream she had dared to dream. In his arms they had all come true. If only love were enough...

A gentle wind blew through her. It scattered wisdom and caution and blew worry like dust before it. The wind grew warmer...hot....

Kyle moved her arms around his neck and embraced her with both his behind her back. His hands roamed her back, slipped down her waist, paused at the curve of her hip, then retreated to her waist. His chest lifted and dropped in a sigh that seemed to blow through her, too.

Their bodies meshed in remembered ways, old but always strangely new. The warmth spread through her until it centered in that secret woman's place deep in her. Her breasts peaked. Her blood throbbed.

Hunger ran like golden sunlight through her. Needs she had fought sprang around her, a meadow of wildflowers, ready to spread their pollen on the wind. The ache shifted and resettled as her body clamored for the release she knew she would find in his arms.

She closed her eyes and rested her cheek on his shoulder. This night…this last night…

They stayed for an hour, then left as the place grew crowded with other couples. The snow was still falling as they made their way to the house.

Inside, she hurried to the bathroom and changed to her warm flannel nightgown. With her face washed and her finery gone, she looked like Cinderella after the clock struck midnight. The ball was over.

When she started for her and Sara's bedroom, she noticed that Kyle had built a fire in the family room. She hesitated, then recalled she hadn't talked to him about the ads Sara was supposed to do.

Maybe this wasn't the time. It was late. They were alone. She should go to bed…alone…

But her feet didn't move toward the bedroom. She walked down the hall. The wood floors were wickedly cold on her feet. But inside she was warm. She felt feverish.

"I forgot to tell you," she began.

He turned from the fire and looked at her.

"I forgot to tell you," she said again.

The words died in her throat. She saw the need, the terrible need that was always in his eyes when he returned home from those dark, scary depths where crime and terror lived. She sensed the cold inside him.

But there was warmth in her. The sun sang in her veins and she was flushed with its heat.

"Dani," he said, the one word spoken low and husky, with an ache inside it.

She pressed her hands to her chest and felt the heat radiating from her body. His soul was dark, lost in an icy wasteland…. She held out her arms.

"Come," she whispered. "I'll warm you. This time. This last time."

"Dani," he murmured and lifted her into his arms.

Chapter Fourteen

Danielle lay in bed and listened to the wind sing around the eaves of the house. Joy and despair sang in her blood. Physically she was satiated and content. But in her soul…

In her soul, her heart, her mind…there's where the ache lay. She thought of the long winters ahead. Perhaps she should have gone south to warmer climes in choosing a new home. She'd once spent a happy vacation in this area. Was she now to spend an unhappy life here?

She closed her eyes against that wild, furious need to weep and envisioned the night. His strong embrace, his delight in her touch, his kisses. He was generous with his kisses, touching each part of her body in the gentlest forays, all the way to her toes.

Heat speared through her. He had driven her to

madness with his kisses, with his skillful caresses. And she had done the same for him, bringing him as much pleasure as she could with her hands, her mouth...

Opening her eyes, she gazed out the window at the gray sky. Clouds again. Snow. Cold.

She sighed and forced herself out of bed. Dressed, she padded into the kitchen in her thick socks. The telephone rang just as she entered. Kyle, seated at the table with the newspaper, grabbed it.

"Hey, Luke," he said after answering.

Luke Mason, his contact for his undercover work with the FBI. A tiny ache pinged through her heart.

"Yeah? Hmm."

She could tell nothing from this end of the conversation. Which was just as well. It didn't matter to her or her future. Kyle was free to go.

"An undercover job? No, thanks."

Her breath caught. She willed herself to normalcy. She poured a cup of coffee and a glass of juice. She took a seat at the table and picked up a section of the paper.

Kyle laughed softly. "Yeah, I've heard your couple-of-weeks argument before."

She stole a glance at him. He was smiling, and his eyes sparkled like sunshine on water. The ache intensified. She would tell him goodbye. She wouldn't cry.

"No way, man. I'm going to stick to the field office." He laughed again. "Tell your problems to Dear Abby. My answer is the same. I'm on R and R."

Then he hung up and settled back in his chair. She stared at the paper, the print a blur before her face.

"Dani," he murmured. "Good morning."

She took a breath, stretched her mouth into a smile and looked at him. His gaze was lambent, tender, all the things she had ever needed from him. She looked at his smiling mouth and thought of all the places he'd touched last night.

Laying the paper aside, she pressed a hand against her chest. She wished they could go back to bed and stay there, content in each other's arms forever.

"Interesting," he said.

"W-what?" She cleared her throat.

"You're blushing like a bride," he commented softly. His gaze drifted over her, sexy and enticing.

She denied it with a quick shake of her head. "Was that Luke Mason?" Such a dumb question and not at all what she wanted to know. "Did he ask you to take an undercover job?"

"Yes, a brief investigation. I turned it down."

"Why?"

"I have a new position lined up. I thought I'd made it clear. I accepted the assignment to the field office."

"Don't," she said. Her voice came out strained, hardly above a whisper.

His eyes narrowed. "Why not?"

"You won't be happy dealing with a lot of paperwork and bureaucrats while your men are out in the field doing the real work. You'll grow to hate it. And Whitehorn."

He was silent for a long time, his gaze fixed on her as if he were looking into her soul. "And you and Sara?"

"You would never hate Sara."

"I would never hate you," he added softly.

She clasped her hands in her lap to still their trembling. "I want you to go. I…it will be easier if you aren't here. I'll share Sara. You're welcome to visit her at any time. She loves hiking and camping out."

"I'm not leaving," he stated.

The hot, hot tears pressed close. She wasn't going to be able to get through this with dignity if he didn't stop arguing. "Please—"

"I've made my choice," he interrupted, his tone still gentle. "I've realized I don't have to save the world all by myself anymore. There are good men and women out there in law enforcement. They can help."

She stared at him, not sure what he was saying.

He smiled, then looked thoughtful. "I've been on a one-person crusade for years. When my mother died I felt guilty, as if it had somehow been my fault."

"She died of cancer. What could you have done?"

"I didn't say it was logical, only that I felt if I had tried harder, been a better person, she might have lived. It was a boy's need, a bargain with God. If He'd let her be okay, I'd do only good all my life. She died, but my guilt didn't, or the need to justify my existence."

Danielle nodded in understanding.

He reached across the table and took her hands in his. "I tried to do good, but there was a darkness in my soul. Sometimes I thought I would sink into it and never come out, that I'd turn into the men I hunted, men with no souls. Then I met you."

A tremor coursed through her at the look in his eyes.

"You, Dani. My light. My guide back to the good world, the real world. When I was on a case, I would lie in bed during the long, lonely nights and look at the moon, but I saw you. It was your light that brightened the night for me. Don't drive me away.''

The tears pressed against her eyes. "Winona said you would always be in law enforcement. It's in your nature.''

He nodded. "I'll still be there. But I'll be the one directing operations. It's the same work but from a different angle. I can let others do the hard stuff. I'm staying with my family.''

The silence spun between them as Kyle gazed deeply into her eyes. He sensed her uncertainty. He'd done that to her.

"If you'll let me,'' he added softly.

She didn't speak.

"Dani.'' It was a plea.

She pushed up from the chair and went to him. He met her halfway. He crushed her into his arms. She crushed back, holding him as tightly as she could.

"If you're sure,'' she whispered. "I couldn't bear it if you wanted to leave, but couldn't.''

"I'm sure.'' He kissed the side of her face, her ear, her neck. "I'm home, Dani, for good. When I wake in the mornings, it's your face I want to see beside me. It's you I want to share life with.'' He pressed his lips against her throat. "In your arms, my sweet shining love, I'm home.''

As Danielle looked into his beautiful eyes, she knew he spoke the truth. "Welcome home, my love.''

* * * * *

*Look out for more **Montana** novels later in the year!*

Silhouette Stars

Born this Month

Elvis Presley, David Bowie, Joan Baez, Rod Stewart, Faye Dunaway, Danny Kay, Kevin Costner, Dolly Parton, Tom Selleck

Star of the Month

Capricorn

There could be opportunities to travel and these may be connected to work. Your love life looks good and there will be many romantic moments to keep the glow in your heart.

SILH/HR/0101a

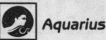

Aquarius

Relationships need careful handling as those close to you may be feeling neglected. Bargain hunting should produce some interesting buys and maybe a new image is what you need.

Pisces

You are enjoying life although you should take care to include loved ones who may be feeling left out. During the course of the month you may have to make an unexpected journey.

Aries

You could be feeling a little jaded so try pampering yourself or getting away for a short break. Career moves look hopeful and you could be appreciated by those who matter.

Taurus

A lucky period in both financial and personal matters. You will be able to start planning a brighter future with confidence. Your success will also rub off on someone close to you.

Gemini

You must make yourself understood if relationships are to get back on a firm footing. Towards the end of the month you should be getting a clearer picture of how to progress.

Cancer

After recent stresses the clouds lift and you will see that happiness is on the horizon. A friend passes on some gossip that will amuse, but take care who you repeat it to.

SILH/HR/0101c

 Leo

You may feel the need to reinvent yourself. However, take care not to leave behind something that really is important. A cash bonus late in the month could trigger a spending spree.

Virgo

Recent disappointments in the romance department have left you wondering about your approach to relationships. By being relaxed and less judgmental, something big is going to happen sooner than you think

 Libra

You must start believing in yourself in order to take advantage of all the wonderful prospects on offer. Romantically an excellent month and a night out brings extra sparkle to your life.

Scorpio

After the excitement of last month life may seem a little quiet. However, use the time to enjoy all you have achieved. Late in the month an interesting proposition may prove tempting.

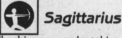 **Sagittarius**

Make an effort to pace yourself; you will achieve more by taking things easy than by rushing around. An unexpected invitation gets you back in the mood to be more social.

**Look out for more
Silhouette Stars next month**

♥™ SILHOUETTE
SPECIAL EDITION®

AVAILABLE FROM 19TH JANUARY 2001

BEGINNING WITH BABY Christie Ridgway

That's My Baby!
When Phoebe Finley needed a 'husband' to keep custody of her adorable infant nephew, strong, sexy Jackson Abbott came to her rescue...

SURPRISE PARTNERS Gina Wilkins

They were just friends and neighbours until they teamed up to avoid the matchmaking antics of their sisters. But their convenient courtship plunged them headlong into inconvenient desire!

FOUND: HIS PERFECT WIFE Marie Ferrarella

It was love at first sight for Alison Quintano when handsome Luc LeBlanc saved her from a mugger, so when he wanted a temporary wife she could not say 'no!'

THEIR LITTLE PRINCESS Susan Mallery

Prescription: Marriage
Earthy single father Tanner Malone breached Dr Kelly Hall's defences and watching him cradle his baby girl made her wish that she could call father and daughter hers...

LONESOME NO MORE Jean Brashear

Perrie Matheson needed refuge from her ex-husband and the Wyoming winter weather. Granite-hard loner Mitch Gallagher's cabin was straight ahead...

A COWBOY'S CODE Alaina Starr

Emma Reardon had transformed herself from a poor farmer's daughter to an independent career woman, and falling for a rancher like Nick Barlow was the last thing she wanted to do.

2 FREE

books and a surprise gift!

We would like to take this opportunity to thank you for reading this Silhouette® book by offering you the chance to take TWO more specially selected titles from the Special Edition™ series absolutely FREE! We're also making this offer to introduce you to the benefits of the Reader Service™—

★ FREE home delivery
★ FREE gifts and competitions
★ FREE monthly Newsletter
★ Exclusive Reader Service discounts
★ Books available before they're in the shops

Accepting these FREE books and gift places you under no obligation to buy, you may cancel at any time, even after receiving your free shipment. Simply complete your details below and return the entire page to the address below. *You don't even need a stamp!*

YES! Please send me 2 free Special Edition books and a surprise gift. I understand that unless you hear from me, I will receive 4 superb new titles every month for just £2.70 each, postage and packing free. I am under no obligation to purchase any books and may cancel my subscription at any time. The free books and gift will be mine to keep in any case.

E1ZEA

Ms/Mrs/Miss/Mr ....Initials.....................................
                                                          BLOCK CAPITALS PLEASE
Surname ....
Address ....
....
....Postcode.....................................

Send this whole page to:
UK: FREEPOST CN81, Croydon, CR9 3WZ
EIRE: PO Box 4546, Kilcock, County Kildare (stamp required)